The
TWO BELLS
OF
Christmas

The
TWO BELLS
OF
Christmas

a regency romance

JOANNA BARKER

An earlier version of the story was published in *A Christmas Promise*,
Timeless Regency Collection Book 16 on November 17, 2020. This is a
newly edited and expanded edition.

Joanna Barker
www.authorjoannabarker.com

First Printing: November 2022

*To everyone who believes
in the magic of Christmas*

CHAPTER 1

Cassandra Bell leaned her head against the cold window, staring out at the bleak and colorless December landscape outside the coach. Well, not colorless, exactly. But the bare trees and dead, dry grass did not inspire any great appreciation for nature at the moment.

A moan came from beside her, and Cassie winced as she turned to her sister. The constant bumping and swaying was enough to make anyone feel ill, but Vivian never traveled well to begin with. She slumped against the side of the coach, eyes glassy and unseeing.

"Are you certain you do not wish to stop?" Cassie asked yet again. Her twin sister's face was as green as the pea soup they'd eaten at the inn while their horses were changed. Though people often had difficulty telling the sisters apart, Cassie doubted anyone would have that trouble today.

Vivian only shook her head in response, gripping the bench beneath her so tightly that her hands turned white.

"You must know that stopping to rest an hour will

hardly hurt your chances of marriage." Cassie attempted a bit of humor—she could always make Vivian smile.

But Vivian did not smile. She gulped a breath, as if desperate for air, and shook her head once again. "No, we cannot stop. We must arrive early."

"Yes, of course," Cassie said dryly. "Because Roland Hastings will surely fall in love with you the moment he sees you looking like a sailor who hasn't yet found his sea legs."

Now Vivian shot her a scowl, though her inability to move without groaning made her infinitely less threatening. "I am certain I will feel better when we arrive at Hartfield Court. But I'll not stop now and lose any chance of spending time with Mr. Hastings before the other ladies arrive."

"Ladies? Tabbies might be the better word."

Vivian's lips twitched. "They certainly will be desperate to sink their claws into poor Mr. Hastings."

"I'm certain Mr. Hastings is many things," Cassie said, "but poor is not one of them." She did not bother to mention that Vivian was acting increasingly like a tabby herself. She was the one, after all, who insisted on arriving as early as possible for the Christmas house party at the Hastings estate, dragging Cassie with her. Now she was on her way to spend the holiday with a group of near strangers, when she would much rather be at home with Grandpapa.

Vivian sighed. "I only wish I knew what inspired the invitation. Was it solely from his mother, or did Mr. Hastings have a hand in it? I doubt he even remembers me at all." She pulled the coach blanket tighter around herself.

The warm brick the coachman had laid at their feet had gone cold hours ago, and the winter chill had crept inside.

"Of course he remembers you," Cassie insisted. "He danced with you twice at the Borlands' ball, and took you in to supper."

He would be more likely to remember Vivian than Cassie, at least. When Papa had introduced them to Mr. Hastings at the ball, Vivian had been ushered to the forefront, as was normal. Cassie had earned nothing more from the gentleman than a brief bow before he'd taken Vivian off to the dance floor. Her first—and only— impression of the man had not been terribly good. He'd seemed aloof, his smile forced and polite.

Vivian had obviously not had the same impression, since she'd been pining after the gentleman since they'd returned from the Season months ago. When the invitation to the house party had arrived, it had caused a celebration the likes of which had not been seen since Wellington's victory at Waterloo.

Vivian looked unconvinced. "I hope you are right, but I am still determined to do what I can to claim his attention. I'll not leave such a thing as love to chance."

Cassie raised an eyebrow. Did her sister's ambitions toward Mr. Hastings truly run so deep? "I think the poets might disagree with that sentiment."

Vivian flapped her hand feebly as she leaned back. "Oh, you know what I mean. I just think Mr. Hastings will need a bit of encouragement, and I should like to offer it first."

"You're more likely to frighten him off than encourage him, the way you're looking now."

Vivian sent her a mock glare. "Any slight about my looks is also against yours."

"Nonsense," Cassie said with a grin. "Everyone knows I'm the prettier twin."

Vivian gave a weak laugh, closing her eyes. "Today that is certainly true."

"Hush now." Cassie tucked her sister's blanket against her. "No more jesting. Try and rest."

Vivian nodded, already half asleep, and Cassie blew out a breath. The next fortnight would be a bore, no doubt, playing her sister's companion as Vivian attempted to entice a proposal from the ever-elusive Mr. Hastings. The invitation had been for Vivian and their mother, but since Mama had been forced to decline due to a younger sister being only weeks from childbirth, Cassie had been sent as a reluctant replacement.

"Do mind yourself," Mama had said reproachfully as Cassie bid her farewell yesterday morning. "Your sister's future depends on this house party, as does yours. If she can make such a conquest as Mr. Roland Hastings, surely you'll soon attract suitors of your own."

"Oh yes, because my foremost requirement for a husband is that he marry me for my family connections."

Mama had not found that particularly funny. "That tongue of yours is precisely why I am uneasy sending you. But as I have no choice, I shall have to hope—nay, pray— you realize behaving yourself is in Vivian's best interest."

Cassie had sighed and kissed her mother on the cheek. "I will bite my tongue, Mama. You needn't worry on my account."

After all, Cassie hardly planned on bringing any

amount of attention to herself during the next fortnight. She would do what she always did during social events: hide when she could and keep her mouth shut when she couldn't. It wasn't that she did not like people, or that she was particularly shy. But experience had proven that if Cassie found something interesting or amusing, Society generally thought the opposite, and she had learned it was better to keep her thoughts to herself.

Cassie jumped as Vivian suddenly sat up straight beside her, grasping the sides of the swaying coach.

"Viv?" Cassie watched her anxiously. "What is wrong?"

Vivian did not answer. She lurched forward and fumbled with the latch on the window, pushing it open and sticking her head out. Then she expelled the contents of her stomach onto the moving scenery outside.

Cassie moved quickly. She snatched her sister's curls back to keep them from blowing across her face, the only help she could offer as Vivian heaved again and again, the coach coming to a stop under the oppressive gray sky.

Lovely. They had yet to set one foot inside Hartfield Court, and already this house party was off to an excellent start.

CHAPTER 2

ROLAND HASTINGS SAT FORWARD in the coach as Hartfield finally came into view through the oak trees lining the drive. He didn't mind London, not really, but his last months there had drained his reserves of patience and energy.

Seeing now the comforting white stone and Grecian columns of his family home in Hampshire brought a relief he hadn't realized he'd been longing for. He leaned back against his seat, the coach rumbling beneath him. At last, some quiet and solitude. And surely Mother had a warm meal waiting for him, even if he had been delayed in London an extra day.

But as they approached the front doors, he spotted an unfamiliar coach already stopped before the steps. That was not surprising in and of itself—his mother was quite popular —though it was late in the day for visitors. What did surprise him was the flurry of activity surrounding the coach as servants unloaded trunks and carried them into the house.

Roland threw open the door and stepped down before the coachman had even brought the equipage to a complete halt. He scaled the steps and marched inside. "Mother?" he called, tugging off his gloves.

No response, but female voices came from down the corridor. He handed a footman his gloves, greatcoat, and hat, then strode to the sitting room, where he found his mother in deep conversation with the housekeeper. Mother's graying dark hair was tucked up inside a mob cap, and she wore a black dress edged in lace. The sight of her made him pause in the doorway. He'd hoped while he'd been gone she might have allowed some gray or lavender back into her wardrobe. But it appeared that a year was still not long enough for her to grieve her husband.

He swallowed hard but stepped forward. "Pardon me, but might I enquire as to whose coach has taken up residence outside?"

Mother looked up, and her eyes brightened. "Roland, you're home!" She stood and embraced him, the smell of her perfume encircling him in a cloud of jasmine and memories.

He allowed her a moment before pulling back and fixing her with a stern look. "You may try and distract me, but I assure you it will not work."

"Hush, you've been gone for months." She tugged his jacket straight. "Allow me to fuss over you a bit."

"Mother . . ."

She stepped back with a sigh and gestured to the housekeeper, who scurried from the room. "Oh, all right.

But it is entirely your fault, arriving home late. I'd planned on more time to tell you."

"Tell me *what?*"

"I've organized a little house party." She waved a hand, as if that would dismiss the sinking sensation in Roland's stomach. "Just a few friends to pass the time until Christmas."

"Until Christmas?" The disbelief in his voice could not begin to match the dismay inside him. "You mean to tell me I've come home anticipating a quiet holiday, and instead I must entertain guests for a fortnight?"

Mama raised her chin. "I've been lonely while you've been away. You cannot deny me some company."

"And you could not have had this company while I was gone?"

She swept back to her chair by the crackling fire. "I was certain you would not wish to miss it."

He gave a short laugh as he ran a hand through his hair. "I think you were certain of the opposite, which is why you did not tell me."

She offered a pained look. "It is hardly my fault you insisted on being a hermit for the last four months."

"I am busy. That does not make me a hermit."

She went on as if he hadn't spoken. "I am only trying to broaden your circle of acquaintances. You'll never meet any ladies of quality if you hole yourself up in your study for weeks on end."

"Ladies?" Roland raised a finger. "Please do not tell me you invited a horde of young women to this house party."

She huffed. "A horde? Do not be ridiculous. I only invited three or four, all accomplished and well-bred."

He nearly threw up his hands. What was she thinking, ambushing him like this? "I am leaving. Going back to London this instant."

His mother straightened, her severe gaze seizing Roland in a vicelike grip. "You most certainly are not," she hissed. "I have put up with your nonsense for long enough. First you carouse your way through the Season, and then you abandon me for months on end."

Roland stepped back. "I haven't abandoned you. You know I had to see to my investments."

"All I know is I have been more than patient, but it is high time you took your responsibilities seriously."

"I have," he insisted. What did she think he'd been doing all that time in London? "The estate is running smoothly, and if all goes well, the return on my new investments will be more than enough to—"

"Not your financial responsibility." Mother clasped her hands in her lap. "Your responsibility to provide an *heir*."

His mouth went dry. Of course. He avoided his mother's eyes and walked to the window, the panes edged in frost. "I'm not yet thirty, Mother. I hardly see that as shirking my duties."

"*If* something does not happen to you." She leaned forward. "What if you suffered an accident and died? You would leave me alone and penniless, forced to relinquish Hartfield to that odious cousin of yours."

Roland sighed. "You would not be penniless, Mother. I know what Father left you."

"That is beside the point. You made a promise, and I intend to make you keep it."

Roland braced his hands against the windowsill as the

memory stole back into his mind. His father lay in bed as Roland clasped his limp hand, his raspy voice insisting that Roland marry and continue the family line. Roland could do nothing but agree. In truth, he'd always known he would marry, so it had seemed an easy thing to promise. That is, until he'd actually made an attempt to find a bride.

"I will marry," Roland said now, still staring out the window. "I promised, and I will."

"Then why can't you see this house party for the opportunity it is?" Mother asked. "I made the invitations very carefully, and I do not think you will find your guests lacking."

He turned to face her. "Who have you invited?"

A triumphant smile leaped across her face. "Miss Tindale and her mother, of course, since you have always been friends."

Friends was perhaps a stretch, but it was true Roland did know the young lady better than most, since their fathers had been good friends in life. But he'd never given her more than a second thought as far as marriage was concerned.

"And?" he prompted, moving to the seat beside hers.

"The Marsdens will be attending, and I must tell you, Miss Marsden has grown quite pretty."

The Marsdens were nearby neighbors, but he couldn't begin to bring an image of Miss Marsden to mind. Was she the timid one with the brown hair? He likely hadn't seen her in over a year.

"And the Bell sisters have just arrived, though I admit I hesitated a bit over that invitation."

Roland looked up. "The Bells? Are they the twins?"

He'd met the Bell family in London last Season and had even danced with Miss Vivian Bell, if he remembered correctly. He had found nothing offensive about her, which was almost unfortunate. He'd hoped to critique his mother's choice in houseguests.

"Yes, the twins." Mother frowned. "I do like the elder Miss Bell, but I cannot say I entirely approve of the younger sister."

"How can you know she is younger? They look exactly the same." He'd had to glance twice at the two sisters when he'd first seen them. Golden-blond hair, bright-blue eyes, and their pert features unnervingly identical.

"I *know*," his mother said coolly. "In any case, I was disappointed to learn that the mother would be unable to attend and that Miss Cassandra would come in her absence. But I assure you you'll find the other young ladies perfectly acceptable." She raised a finger. "And you will treat them well, no matter that you did not want them here."

A shrill meow came from behind him, and his mother's cat, Sir Chester, came slinking into the room. The black and white creature had always hated Roland, and clearly its feelings had not changed in the last few months. It watched him with narrow, yellow eyes as it crossed the room and leaped onto Mother's lap. She stroked its back distractedly, still eyeing Roland.

Roland crossed his arms, not wanting to give in so easily, not when he knew she must have been planning this for months. "I won't be rude to our guests," he said. "I am civilized enough for that."

"I want more than civility, Roland." Mother's voice softened unexpectedly. "I want you to *try*."

He was half tempted to give a cheeky retort, but he stopped himself. She only wanted the best for him, even if he didn't at all agree with her methods.

"Let us make an arrangement then," he said finally. "If I promise to allow this house party a chance, *you* must promise that if nothing comes of it, you'll let me be. You will not attempt to play matchmaker in the future."

Mother considered his offer, then nodded. "Very well. I accept your terms. But know I will be watching."

He groaned. "Yes, because nothing encourages romance like the watchful eye of a potential mother-in-law."

She picked up the paper she'd been perusing when he'd arrived, one hand still stroking Sir Chester's back. "You'll manage somehow, I am sure. Now go and dress for dinner. Our other guests will arrive shortly."

"Very well," he said. "But come Christmas, I expect to have my house back."

Mother only gave a sly smile. "Hopefully with one new addition."

He blew out a frustrated breath as he left the room and started up the main staircase. Was there a worse way to spend Christmas than an entire fortnight with three young women determined to pry a proposal from him?

He would not come away unscathed, of that he was certain.

CHAPTER 3

OF ONE THING Cassie was absolutely certain: her sister had gone mad.

Though Vivian had spent the last two hours of their journey alternatively moaning or sticking her head out the window, she now slumped weakly in an armchair as she and Jennings—their shared lady's maid—deliberated over dresses.

"No, not that one," she said, her voice faint. "Try the white."

Jennings set down the blue gown and rifled through the trunk.

Cassie rubbed her forehead. "You cannot be serious, Viv. Mama wouldn't let you attend dinner tonight in your condition, and neither shall I."

"I am just a bit queasy from the ride, that's all," Vivian said even as she clenched the arms of the chair in her shaking hands.

"This is more than a bit of queasiness," Cassie insisted.

"I think you might be truly ill. Can we not send for a doctor?"

When the sisters had arrived at Hartfield Court a half hour ago, Vivian had said nothing of her illness. Instead, she'd plastered a smile on her face while greeting Mrs. Hastings. As soon as the housekeeper had shown them their rooms, she had collapsed in a chair and hadn't stood since.

"I cannot see a doctor." Vivian's voice had taken on a strange insistence. "I need to attend dinner tonight."

"You can barely stand." Cassie strode to Jennings and took the white silk evening gown from her hands. "You certainly cannot endure an entire evening of entertainment and socializing, even in the name of love."

A knock came at the door, and the housekeeper peeked inside the room. "Pardon, Miss Cassandra, but your trunk has been brought to your room."

"Thank you." Cassie was desperate to change into something that did not smell like—well, like retch. She turned back to her sister. "Will you please lie down until I change, at least? Then I might stop planning your funeral."

Vivian sighed. "Very well. For a few minutes."

After helping Vivian to the canopied bed and tucking her into the blankets, Cassie went to the room the housekeeper had shown her when they'd arrived. Closing the door behind her, Cassie hurried to the trunk set at the foot of the bed. She undid the latches and propped open the lid, then stared. Her eyes were met not by petticoats and stockings, but by white linen shirts, bold-colored waistcoats, and a stack of neatly pressed handkerchiefs.

She took up a handkerchief. What on earth? She

stepped back and inspected the trunk. It looked like hers at first glance, but no, the leather was a darker color, and the buckles more gold than bronze. The footmen must have confused her trunk for someone else's, another guest arriving for the party, surely. Her trunk was likely waiting in another room, hopefully untouched by the gentleman who owned this trunk.

Gentleman. Cassie's face heated, and she slammed shut the trunk before she saw anything scandalous. She hurried back into the corridor, intent on finding the housekeeper. But halfway to the stairs, a door flung open in front of her. She yelped and threw out her hands to stop it from smashing into her face.

"Blast," said a masculine voice, and a man stepped from behind the door. Dark hair, thick brows, and the deep-brown eyes that had entranced half of London during the Season. "I'm terribly sorry. Are you all right?"

Cassie shook out her hands, still stinging from slamming against the hard wood of the door. "I'd be better if you hadn't nearly broken my nose." Did Mr. Hastings always run around throwing open doors haphazardly?

He winced. "My apologies. Miss Bell, is it?" Then he squinted at her. "Or is it Miss Cassandra?"

She could hardly be annoyed with him for being unable to tell her and Vivian apart. No one could, save for their parents and a few close friends. But she wasn't yet reconciled to forgiveness.

"Cassandra," she said coolly, offering a brief curtsy. "A pleasure, Mr. Hastings, but I'm afraid there has been some mix-up and—"

His eyes wandered to her hand, where she still

clutched the handkerchief from the trunk, and he nodded unexpectedly. "Ah, I think I've solved the mystery. Might I guess that your trunk does not contain your usual belongings? Mine was shockingly filled with ruffles and lace."

Cassie blanched. Had Mr. Hasting rifled through her things? "You didn't—"

He held up his hands. "I did not touch a thing, though that is more than you can say."

The handkerchief itched in her hand, as if accusing her. She held it out to him immediately. "I thought it might identify the owner."

He took it. "Success. Shall we correct this mistake?"

She expected him to call for a footman to switch the trunks, but he instead disappeared back through the doorway. Cassie reluctantly followed him down a short corridor to what she assumed was his room. She peered inside as he went to the trunk—*her* trunk—and hefted it into his arms. Rather easily, she admitted reluctantly.

"Now, which room is yours?" he said, carefully maneuvering through the doorway.

Cassie started down the corridor, and he followed with heavy footsteps. She glanced back to find him already watching her with narrowed eyes. She cleared her throat. "Pardon my asking, Mr. Hastings, but are you only now arriving?"

When they'd arrived earlier, she hadn't thought to wonder about his absence when Mrs. Hastings had greeted them. She'd been far too concerned with helping a staggering Vivian to her room, barely avoiding a repeat performance of the incident in the coach.

But now she was curious. If he *had* just arrived, then she doubted he'd played any role in inviting Vivian to the house party.

Mr. Hastings frowned. "Yes, I was delayed in London, and I'm afraid a great many unexpected obstacles have made their way into my life today."

Did he mean their trunks? It seemed such a small thing to make him frown so. But Cassie refrained from saying anything more. If Vivian was successful in her endeavor, this man would be her future brother-in-law. She hardly wanted him thinking worse of her than he already did, considering he already assumed she'd ransacked his trunk.

"Here it is," she said as they stepped into her room. She gestured at the open trunk. "As you can see, I did not touch anything beside the handkerchief."

He sent her an odd look as he set her trunk on the floor. "I hope you know I was only joking about that."

"Oh." She cleared her throat. "Well, good. Thank you for your help, Mr. Hastings."

He raised an eyebrow at her dismissal but did not protest as he lifted his trunk. "Of course, Miss Cassandra."

He made his way back to the door, and she moved to her trunk, wanting to reassure herself that all was in order.

"By the way," Mr. Hastings called from the doorway. She looked up. "I am also quite fond of cherry comfits." He flashed a grin and vanished down the corridor, leaving her staring after him.

Then her eyes dropped to her trunk, and she opened

it. She thought she'd carefully packed her brown-paper package from the apothecary, but apparently the wrapping had come loose during the journey, and the small sweets wrapped in twists of paper had spilled all over her trunk.

"Drat," she muttered. She began scooping up the comfits and depositing them on the nearby writing desk. Now Mr. Hastings thought her a snoop *and* a glutton. Mama would be so proud.

When her trunk was free of sweets, she changed quickly, accustomed to dressing without help since Vivian often monopolized Jennings's time. Then she hurried back to her sister's room.

"I must tell you," she said, slipping inside. "I just had the strangest meeting—"

Cassie stopped. Vivian was not resting on the bed. Instead, her sister sat beside the chamber pot on the floor, leaning her head against the wall.

"Oh, Vivian." Cassie went to her and helped her sit on the edge of the bed. Where had Jennings gone? "You cannot still be thinking of going down to dinner."

"No," Vivian said, still pale. "I think it is very clear I cannot."

"Good." Finally she was seeing reason. "Now you must—"

"But *you* can," Vivian interrupted.

Cassie crossed her arms. "There is no point in me going down. *I* haven't set my cap for anyone, and I would rather stay with you." Truthfully, Cassie was relieved. Now she had the perfect excuse to miss the first evening of the house party. Who would insist she play parlor games when she was needed to nurse her dear sister back to health?

But Vivian only shook her head, a look of determination claiming her eyes. "Cassie, I need your help."

Cassie squinted at her. "Of course. That is why I want to stay with you."

"No, you do not understand." Vivian's arms were trembling. "We need to switch."

"Switch?" Cassie dropped her arms. "Why?"

They hadn't switched places in years, not since they'd found it amusing to trick their horrible French governess. And of course they'd done it endless times as young girls, to the exasperation of their mother, but it had only ever been in fun.

Vivian took a deep breath. "You know how I feel about Mr. Hastings, and what my hopes are. But . . ." She swallowed. "But if I cannot be there tonight, I may as well give up now. Miss Tindale is everything that is charming, beautiful, and accomplished."

"So are you," Cassie insisted. "Mr. Hastings knows this." Despite her words, she was far from certain. He hadn't looked particularly thrilled to see Cassie in the hallway, even for the short second he thought she was Vivian.

Vivian ignored her. "You must pretend to be me and ensure that Miss Tindale does not entirely commandeer Mr. Hastings."

"And why can't I do that as myself?" Cassie asked, propping one fist on her hip. "I can distract him just as well without going through all this pretense."

"Because I need to maintain my reputation," she

insisted. "Who wishes to marry a sickly girl who hides away in her bedchamber?"

"I see," Cassie said dryly. "So instead, Cassandra Bell will be the sickly girl who hides away in her bedchamber."

"But you do not care what people think of you."

That was true, for the most part. But somehow it made Cassie uneasy, that the peculiar Mr. Hastings would think of her that way.

"Please?" Vivian begged. "It would just be for tonight. You know I never stay ill for long. We can both rejoin the party tomorrow."

"This is ridiculous." Cassie rubbed her forehead. "You cannot be serious."

"Why not? No one can tell us apart."

Cassie threw up her hands. "We are not fourteen years old anymore, Viv. There is no possible way I can convince an entire household, not when they already know the *real* you."

"Of course you can," Vivian said, though her voice was fading. "You know me better than anyone."

"That does not mean I can *be* you."

"But you must. This is too important." Then Vivian's eyebrows lifted. "Think, Cassie. If I am married before the Season, you needn't go to London."

That gave Cassie pause. They both knew very well that Mama had only brought Cassie to London because leaving her at home while parading Vivian around would have sparked rumors. But Vivian was the daughter on whom their parents had pinned their hopes for a great match—which, of course, Cassie was perfectly content with. She hardly wanted *more* attention.

And while London had been all good and well in its own way—the food and entertainment, at least—she could certainly do without it. *Especially* if it meant avoiding awkward dances with men she hardly knew or tagging along on never-ending social visits. She much preferred their quiet country home and the company of Grandpapa. He was the only one who laughed rather than cringed when Cassie said something absurd.

If Cassie did what Vivian wanted . . . if she could succeed in helping her sister secure a match with Mr. Hastings . . .

Vivian's shoulders slumped as her energy waned.

"You are going to faint," Cassie said, moving closer. "Lie down."

Vivian jutted her chin. "Not until you promise you'll do it."

Cassie blew out a breath. How could she even be considering this? Vivian was proper and lovely and good. Cassie was . . . not. But could she pretend for long enough to salvage Vivian's hopes for the future?

"One night," she finally said. "I will go to dinner tonight."

Vivian flung her arms around Cassie, who staggered under her sister's weight. "Oh, thank you. I knew you would agree."

"Now into bed with you," Cassie ordered. She helped Vivian to lie back and pulled the blankets up tight around her chin. "And *you* must promise to let me call for a doctor if you are still unwell tomorrow."

"I promise," Vivian said solemnly.

Cassie exhaled, crossing her arms. "This will end in disaster, you must know that."

"Of course it won't." Vivian closed her eyes, as if their conversation had exhausted her completely. Which it likely had. "You'll be perfect, I have no doubt."

No matter. Cassie had enough doubts for the both of them.

CHAPTER 4

THE SECOND ROLAND stepped into the drawing room, he regretted agreeing to his mother's ridiculous plan.

All eyes turned to him. Mr. and Mrs. Marsden and their daughter—who *was* the timid, brown-haired girl he'd vaguely remembered. Miss Tindale and her hawkeyed mother, who stood in the corner, separate from the others. And Mother, of course, who presided over it all with a careful determination.

Roland squared his shoulders and forced a smile. He greeted each guest in turn, making a special effort to converse with both Miss Marsden and Miss Tindale as his mother would want. It wasn't their fault she had arranged this entire debacle, after all. That was also why he'd forced himself to be polite when he'd met Miss Cassandra in the upstairs corridor earlier, even when she'd practically accused him of sorting through her petticoats.

Though he hadn't been able to resist that last parting shot about her large stash of comfits. He'd rather enjoyed the embarrassment that flashed across her face.

He glanced around the drawing room. Where *were* the Bell sisters?

"How was your journey from London, Mr. Hastings?"

Miss Tindale came to his side, smiling brightly as she tipped her head, her brown curls framing her heart-shaped face. Once he might have been immediately taken in by such a pretty face. But after last Season, after months of dancing and flirting and talking, after making every effort to find a woman he could build a life with . . .

Now he was more cautious—and realistic. He'd almost given up the idea of marriage entirely and decided to focus on his work instead, but if these young ladies would be staying at his home for a fortnight, then he might as well follow through on his promise to Mother. He still wanted to marry; he just wasn't certain the Fates agreed with him.

Now he forced a smile to his face. "My journey was excellent. And yours, Miss Tindale?"

"Oh, perfectly lovely. I so enjoy traveling, and the countryside here is beautiful."

He almost laughed. The landscape was drab and bleak in the middle of December. But she was only being gracious. He could hardly fault her for it.

"Are you looking forward to Christmas, Mr. Hastings?" Miss Tindale asked. "I admit I've never been particularly fond of the holiday, but surely your mother has a host of wonderful things planned for us all."

"Yes, I am certain—" he began.

"Good evening!"

The high, breathy voice interrupted him, and he turned to see a halo of golden curls and vivid sky-blue eyes. "Mr. Hastings, Miss Tindale," the young lady said, dropping two bobbing curtsies in quick succession.

"Ah, Miss . . ." He hesitated. "Miss Cassandra, is it?"

She shook her head quickly, as if eager to correct him. "No, sir, I am Vivian."

So this was Miss Vivian Bell. Blast, it was a dreadful task to keep the two of them sorted out. "And where is your sister?" he asked.

"I'm afraid Cassandra is feeling ill today." Miss Bell clasped her gloved hands. "You shall have to make due with just me."

Roland squinted. "Ill? But I saw her only a few hours ago. She looked perfectly well to me."

"Oh?" Miss Bell's eyes widened almost alarmingly. "How odd. I think the journey simply did not agree with her. I daresay she'll be recovered by tomorrow."

At least that would make the sisters easier to keep track of in the meantime. Not that he wished the younger Miss Bell to be sick. In fact, he had almost begun to anticipate meeting her again, to see if she might say anything about their earlier interactions. But it was better this way. After all, Vivian was the one his mother had specifically invited for him.

"How good to see you again, Miss Bell." Miss Tindale slipped seamlessly into the conversation. "I am sorry to hear about your sister, but so long as her condition is not serious, I hope she can join us soon enough."

"Yes, of course," Miss Bell said, and then stood with her mouth slightly parted, as if she knew she ought to say something else, but could not quite manage it. She glanced around. "This room is lovely. I like the—the

25

colors. And the windows." She shifted her weight. "Of course, Miss Tindale, you look lovely as well, with your . . ." She wafted a hand over her own head, indicating that she meant Miss Tindale's elaborate hairstyle enhanced by two tall, white feathers. "And Mr. Hastings, you look—" She broke off, clearly struggling for words. "You also look lovely?"

She had used the word *lovely* thrice in the span of twenty seconds. And he wasn't certain he had ever heard the term applied to a man.

"Thank you, Miss Bell," he said, casting a confused look at Miss Tindale. She, of course, was too practiced in the ways of society to show any reaction save for a slight arch to her eyebrow.

They were all saved from further interaction by Mrs. Hastings's announcement that dinner was ready. Roland excused himself and moved to escort the matronly Mrs. Marsden into dinner, as was proper, yet he could not help a glance back. Miss Tindale had rejoined her mother, but Miss Bell stood with her hands on her waist, shoulders slumped. As he watched, she let out short puff of air from the side of her mouth, blowing a curl from her face. Then she met his eyes. She straightened suddenly, as if he had caught her doing something rather wicked.

During the Season, Roland had spent—at most—a few hours with Miss Vivian Bell, and he had assessed her to be everything society wished for in a young lady: poised, proper, and polite. But tonight it seemed as though something had set the young lady on edge.

Though, of course, this entire house party could certainly be reason enough. Roland was unsure if Miss

Bell, Miss Tindale, and Miss Marsden knew precisely why they'd been invited, but they had to at least suspect. What was he to do, court all three in the hopes that one would somehow be all he was searching for in a wife?

He pushed back those thoughts as he offered his arm to Mrs. Marsden. He could not think that far ahead. He *could* be kind and polite and everything his mother wished him to be.

At least for two weeks.

Dinner was *not* going well.

First, Cassie sat too quickly as the footman pushed her chair in, and she almost dropped to the floor. Thankfully, she caught herself on the edge of the table, and no one noticed. Then she spilled her glass of wine and stained the white tablecloth nearly the entire length of the table, which *everyone* noticed, though Mrs. Hastings assured her it was nothing.

Why on earth had she agreed to this switch? Her nerves were as frayed as her favorite shawl. She never felt entirely comfortable in company on a normal day, but neither was she ever this incompetent. At this rate, she would out her own charade in an attempt to save her sanity.

She steadied herself with deep breaths. Vivian needed Cassie to make this work. And Cassie needed it too, if she was to avoid another tiresome Season in London.

Thankfully, she was seated beside Mrs. Tindale, who was far too focused on her daughter across the table to speak to Cassie. Miss Tindale had somehow managed to secure a seat near Mr. Hastings and had claimed his attention for most of dinner.

Which, Cassie realized belatedly, was exactly the sort of thing she was supposed to prevent while playing Vivian. She'd been so caught up in her fears of being found out that she'd forgotten her purpose. When at last Mrs. Hastings rose to lead the women from the dining room, Cassie followed with new determination. She would do what Vivian would do. She would not let Miss Tindale dominate the drawing room as she had dinner.

And she would *not* use the word *lovely*.

Cassie passed an awkward few minutes making conversation with the shy Miss Marsden, who somehow seemed more uncomfortable than Cassie. Was she always like this? Surely she wasn't also pretending to be her twin sister.

The men joined them rather quickly, which was unsurprising, as the male portion of the party included only Mr. Hastings and the elder Mr. Marsden. As soon as Mr. Hastings stepped inside the drawing room, Cassie excused herself and moved to intercept him. But before she could take two steps, Miss Tindale swooped in like a falcon after a mouse. How could she move so fast and yet so gracefully? Cassie pushed her chin up a notch. She would not back away. She joined the two of them as Miss Tindale began questioning him about the landscape painting that hung above the fireplace.

"That is our family house in Yorkshire," Mr. Hastings said, clasping his hands behind his back. "Willow Cottage."

"The artist is quite talented," Miss Tindale said. "What pretty colors. I daresay it is something of a masterpiece."

Cassie examined the painting. Were Miss Tindale's eyes going dim? "I would hardly call it a masterpiece," she said. Now was Cassie's chance to set herself apart from the other ladies. "Why, if the house was actually at that scale compared to the coach, even a child would be hard-pressed to make it through the doorways. And the sheep look a bit more like clouds with legs rather than animals."

If Cassie had thought she might impress with her detailed critique, she was quickly proven wrong as she was met by silence and bewilderment.

Mr. Hastings gave a slight cough. "This painting was done by my mother."

Oh, dear.

"That is," Cassie said frantically, "the brushstrokes are skillfully done, as is the general . . . uh . . . landscape." She had *told* Vivian this would be a disaster.

But perhaps Mrs. Hastings had not heard. Cassie glanced behind her—and was met by the woman's fierce scowl from where she sat not ten feet away. Drat. Never mind the spilt wine—she'd gone and insulted the mother of the man her sister hoped to marry.

"*I* think it a beautiful painting," Miss Tindale said smoothly. "If the actual Willow Cottage is half so pretty as its rendering here, I should be very pleased to see it one day."

Miss Tindale sent Cassie a knowing smile. Of course. The minx must have known Mrs. Hastings had painted the picture—hence why she'd complimented it in the first place.

But Cassie held her tongue. She'd already done enough damage to Vivian's reputation tonight as it was.

Miss Tindale turned the conversation to other topics, and Cassie slipped away and retreated to the far corner of the room, where the cold and dark leeched through the windows as she sat primly on a chair. If she could keep herself far enough away . . .

"Are you determined to exile yourself, then?"

Cassie jerked her head up. Mr. Hastings had followed her across the room, leaving everyone else staring in his wake, though they tried to pretend otherwise. He stood beside her, his eyes amused.

She cleared her throat. "Only until I learn a bit of prudence."

"Prudence is all good and well," he said, taking the chair beside hers. "But so is honesty. And I must admit I've often thought the same thing of the cloud sheep."

"I appreciate you voicing your opinion now, rather than two minutes ago," Cassie said dryly.

Mr. Hastings grinned. "Never mind my mother. She'll have forgotten by tomorrow."

Cassie highly doubted that, but then it wasn't *his* head Mrs. Hastings was currently glaring daggers at.

"Be that as it may," she said, "I think it best to keep my head down."

He leaned back in his chair. "Probably wise for the moment. My mother has never been one to enjoy criticism."

"Does anyone?"

"No, I suppose not." Mr. Hastings wore a thoughtful

expression. "Tell me, Miss Bell, what qualifies you to appraise artwork? Are you a painter?"

She almost laughed, but she managed to cut the sound off with a cough. No, Cassie was not a painter. But Vivian was. The only reason Cassie had even thought to mention the flaws of Mrs. Hastings's painting was because of the many hours her sister had dragged her from museum to museum in London.

"Yes, I paint," she said. Was it a lie if it *was* true about Vivian? Cassie hadn't had time to untangle the moral ambiguities of what she was doing. "Though from my unkind words about your mother's painting, you might assume a higher level of expertise than I actually possess. I am nothing more than a mildly talented artist with a lack of tact."

"As I have no artistic inclinations whatsoever, you still claim an advantage over me." He tipped his head. "And what do you like to paint?"

"Oh." She paused. Why was he pursuing this conversation? She'd just made a fool of herself in front of the entire party. Did he feel sorry for her, or perhaps feel as if he owed her time, having already spent a good portion of the evening with Miss Tindale? "I paint a bit of everything, I suppose." Cassie tried to remember which subjects filled Vivian's canvases most often. "Landscapes, flowers, animals."

"Animals?"

"Yes, we've something of a menagerie at Brightling Place. My father breeds hunting dogs, and many of our tenants also raise sheep and goats. And of course there is the parrot."

Mr. Hastings raised an eyebrow. "Why, of course. Because what country estate is complete without a parrot?"

Cassie laughed. "It belongs to my grandfather. He purchased it from a sailor who seemed desperate to be rid of it, for reasons that soon became obvious."

"You are keeping me in suspense, Miss Bell."

Miss Bell. It shouldn't feel so strange to be addressed as such. It *was* Cassie's name too, after all. But as the older sister, Vivian had always been Miss Bell.

Cassie cleared her throat. "We soon learned that the bird knew only a few phrases and repeated them with unbridled enthusiasm—which would not have been so terrible if the phrases had been more . . . appropriate."

Mr. Hastings's lips twitched. "You are saying the parrot dared to use unsuitable language in front of a young lady?"

"*Dares.*" Cassie emphasized the present tense. "My grandfather loves the old bird too much to be rid of it. He used to travel a great deal as a young man, and I believe the parrot helps him relive those times."

Talking of Grandpapa caused an acute ache in Cassie's chest. She'd left Brightling only two days before, but she already missed him dreadfully. There was no one she felt more free with, more herself—save for Vivian, of course. Although lately Cassie felt as though even Vivian was drifting farther away, especially since the Season. Marriage had become of the utmost importance to her, and Cassie could not quite summon the same enthusiasm.

"You are fond of your grandfather." Mr. Hastings

watched her with a curious sharpness, one hand rubbing his chin.

"Yes," she said hesitantly. Why did it feel as if their conversation had suddenly turned into an odd sort of test? "Very much so."

He smiled, and Cassie's heartbeat took an unexpected tumble. He *was* handsome, after all, with that dark hair and those brown eyes, long lashes, and sharp cheekbones. Had she never looked at the man closely before? Or had she convinced herself that Society thought too highly of him and dismissed him without real consideration?

"Or perhaps," he said, "you are simply fond of your grandfather's improper parrot."

Cassie did like the silly parrot—she thought it rather hilarious. But *Vivian* did not. Or at least she did not laugh anymore when Grandpapa brought the bird into the drawing room after dinner. She always looked more like Mama, who clenched her jaw with every word that escaped the parrot's mouth.

"I . . ." Cassie hesitated. She'd already shown Mr. Hastings perhaps a bit too much of her own personality tonight. She needed to let Vivian take control now. "I admit I did like it when I was younger. But now I find its language disconcerting, especially as I aspire to absolute propriety."

There. That ought to help Vivian's image.

But it seemed to have the opposite effect. Mr. Hastings straightened, and the gleam in his eyes disappeared. "Yes, of course," he said. "I would never insinuate you are less than ladylike."

"No, I did not mean—"

He shook his head. "No matter. I understand." He stood and offered a brief smile. "My mother needs me."

Indeed, his mother was gesturing at him across the room, her scowl from earlier gone, though the hard lines around her eyes remained.

Mr. Hasting offered a short bow, and for a moment his expression softened. "I hope we have more time to talk during the party, Miss Bell. I look forward to knowing you better."

Heat crept across her cheeks. Cassie seldom blushed, but that was due to the rarity of a man's attention more than any other reason. "As do I," she managed with a nod.

He left to rejoin his mother, and Cassie tried not to let her eyes linger on his shoulders, his tall frame, as he walked away.

She did not succeed.

CHAPTER 5

"You must tell me everything." Vivian propped herself up on shaking arms, her face pale, as Cassie slipped into her room later that night. "This instant."

"Can it wait until morning?" Cassie pulled pins from her hair, letting her curls loose from their tight constraints. "It is exhausting pretending to be you. How can you be *so* proper all the time?"

Vivian ignored her. "Please. Tell me. Did it work?"

Cassie sat on the bed beside her sister. "For the most part, though you may not thank me for it after hearing the details."

She summarized the evening, from her idiotic *lovelies* to her insult of Mrs. Hastings's artwork.

"And that is why," she concluded, as if presenting a scientific lecture to the Royal Society, "we should never have attempted this in the first place. I only made things worse."

Vivian leaned back, her eyes thoughtful. "Possibly.

Well, certainly with Mrs. Hastings. But I can smooth her ruffled feathers with little issue tomorrow."

"If you are well tomorrow," Cassie pointed out. "You do not look the least bit improved. Are you certain this is just from traveling?"

"Quite," Vivian said, though her trembling voice negated her answer. "But what matters is that you were able to distract Mr. Hastings from Miss Tindale."

"Undoubtedly." If looking ridiculous at a dinner party was her ticket to returning home, then she would happily make that sacrifice.

"What did you and Mr. Hastings talk about?" Vivian asked, rubbing her forehead with a wince.

"Nothing of great consequence, I assure you." Cassie frowned, watching her sister. If Vivian was not better by tomorrow, she would insist upon a doctor.

"I must know everything," Vivian said, "so we may transition back seamlessly tomorrow. He cannot know you were pretending to be me."

Cassie sighed. She was right, of course. "We talked of your love of painting."

Vivian nodded.

"And I mentioned Grandpapa's parrot."

Vivian stopped nodding. "The parrot? You cannot be serious."

Cassie shrugged. "It made for interesting conversation."

"But the parrot." Vivian groaned. "That foul creature should have no part in a drawing room, even just in conversation."

"It isn't foul." Cassie straightened. "It is amusing."

Vivian fell back on her pillows. "At least I know you spoke of it, in case Mr. Hastings mentions it."

Cassie shook her head. "Viv, you should not worry about this now. Rest, please."

"All right." Vivian did not resist very hard. "But do not let me sleep all morning. I am determined to go to breakfast."

"Of course." At least this lie was easy for Cassie to make, knowing it was for her sister's good.

If only it could be the last lie she told.

Vivian was worse the next morning.

Upon finding her sister barely able to raise her head, Cassie went to Mrs. Hastings immediately—acting as Vivian, of course—and asked for a doctor. Fortunately, the matron complied without complaint, though she watched Cassie with narrowed eyes.

When Dr. Dutton arrived, he examined Vivian carefully. Cassie took up position at his elbow.

"Can you say what it is, Doctor?" Cassie finally asked. "Nothing serious, I hope?"

The doctor shook his head as he felt Vivian's pulse. "I'm afraid I cannot be certain. She has a fever, but it is not dangerously high. I have seen similar symptoms in other patients recently, and all recovered within a few days."

"A few days?" Vivian paled even more, which Cassie had thought impossible. "I cannot be abed that long. In fact, I need to dress now if I'm to be ready for breakfast."

She began to rise from the bed, but Dr. Dutton set a gentle hand on her shoulder.

"I'm afraid that will only make things worse," he said. "For your own sake, and for the sake of others, I insist you remain in bed until I pronounce you well enough."

Vivian sank back against her pillows. "This is ridiculous."

Dr. Dutton went to his bag and gathered his instruments. "I'll come again this afternoon to see her," he said to Cassie. "Keep her in bed, and send for me if her condition changes."

Cassie nodded and the doctor left. She turned back to Vivian, who scowled at the ceiling. "I'm sorry," she said, and she meant it. Even if she thought her sister's plan of wooing Mr. Hastings rather silly, she never wanted to see Vivian distressed.

"A few days," Vivian repeated again, defeated. "It is utterly useless. By the time I am well again, Miss Tindale will have ensured that no one remembers I exist."

Cassie sat beside her. "Never mind that. We must get you well first. I promise you'll have your chance."

"Yes, you are right," Vivian said slowly, fixing Cassie with a meaningful look. "But until then . . ."

Cassie straightened. Then she held up her hands. "No. No and no."

"But it is the only way," Vivian pled. "Can't you see? If you simply continue the switch for another few days, no one will be the wiser."

"I was the worst possible Vivian Bell last night," Cassie said stubbornly. "You cannot want that to continue."

"I can, since it is my only option. Besides, you'll grow

better at it, I am sure." Vivian took her hand, squeezing it tightly. "Please, Cassie? Just a bit longer. Let me have my chance at happiness."

Cassie knew she should say no. Heavens, she should pretend to be sick right alongside Vivian so she could avoid the rest of the party.

But Vivian looked at her with such desperation. Cassie had never been able to refuse her sister in anything, and this was so important to her. Not to mention, if Cassie *was* successful . . . She pictured a cozy Christmas back at Brightling, happily tucked away for the winter with no dread for the upcoming Season.

"All right," Cassie said with a long exhale. "I'll do it."

Vivian patted her hand. "Thank you, Cassie. It will be done before you know it." Her eyes widened. "But hurry, you must go down to breakfast before everyone disperses. I am absolutely certain Miss Tindale has already cornered Mr. Hastings."

A few minutes later, dressed in Vivian's flowered morning gown, Cassie descended the main staircase, trying to find the confidence she would need. She could do this, she told herself. She knew Vivian better than anyone.

"Good morning, Miss Bell."

Cassie jumped, but it was only Miss Tindale striding across the entry, her lovely dark locks arranged into a simple chignon.

"Oh. Good morning." Cassie cleared her throat. "Have I missed breakfast?"

Miss Tindale smiled pleasantly. Well, as pleasantly as a vulture could manage. "They haven't cleared it away yet, but you might hurry." Then her smile turned sympathetic. "How is your dear Cassandra? I understand the doctor was called for this morning."

"She is . . ." Cassie paused. She was technically speaking of herself, and she hardly wanted to add to her sickly reputation. "She should be well enough to join us in a day or two." Perhaps if Cassie wished *very* hard, her words would come true.

"That is good news. Do give her my best wishes." Miss Tindale gave the barest curtsy and brushed past Cassie to reach the stairs.

"And where are you off to in such a hurry?" The words slipped from Cassie's mouth before she could stop them.

Miss Tindale turned back. "Have you not heard? Mrs. Hastings has lost her cat, and she is simply distraught. I am helping in the search efforts, of course. Anything for sweet Mrs. Hastings."

Sweet as codfish. At least Cassie managed to stop *those* words.

"That is very kind of you," she said instead. But she knew it was more than kindness at play. Whoever found this cat would undoubtedly be in Mrs. Hastings's good graces, and Miss Tindale was planning to take that coveted position.

Unless Cassie found the feline first.

She bid farewell to Miss Tindale and started for the breakfast room, but as soon as the young lady disappeared upstairs, Cassie veered down the ground floor corridor. Eating could wait; winning back her hostess's approval could not.

She searched the library, the dining room, the sitting

room, and the billiards room. But after half an hour, Cassie was no closer to finding the creature than she was to flying. She stopped in the middle of the billiards room, hands on her waist. If *she* were a cat desperate to escape an unpleasant and judgmental mistress, where would she go?

A blur of movement caught her eye outside the window. Cassie crossed the room and pulled back the curtains just as a curved gray tail slipped around the corner of the stables.

She dropped the curtain and nearly ran for the door.

CHAPTER 6

ROLAND KICKED HIS HORSE, urging his stallion faster as they galloped up the frost-covered hill, the bright winter sun throwing shadows behind the bare trees. If a houseful of guests made him tug on his too-stiff collar, a brisk ride in the chill December air had the opposite effect. His blood pounded through him, filling him with a heat he hadn't felt in months. Riding in Hyde Park was not the same as taking the countryside in hand, mastering the land as he and his mount jumped hedges and waded through streams.

But of course he couldn't do this all day, as much as he wished to. He'd never hear the end of it from Mother if he avoided the party for much longer. He'd already skipped breakfasting with the guests in favor of a tray in his room. Although, if he was being honest, he wasn't quite sure who he was intent on avoiding. Miss Tindale had proven an apt conversationalist at dinner last night, which somewhat refreshing after his experience with the majority of vain, single-minded women in London.

And yet, he admitted, it was not her face that came to mind when he thought of last night. No, instead of Miss Tindale's dark hair and porcelain complexion, he saw golden curls and laughing blue eyes.

Roland turned his horse back toward the house, his breath leaving clouds in his wake. Miss Bell had proven a surprise last night, with her dry repartee and entertaining tales of the foul-mouthed parrot. When he tried to remember her in London, he could not recall much at all, save for the fact that he hadn't found himself immediately drawn to her. That had been enough for him then, but now he could not help but think he had dismissed her too quickly.

After entering the stables, Roland dismounted and handed his reins to a waiting groom. But as he strode toward the door, he came to a sudden halt. There, in the open stall across the way, was the focus of his thoughts: Miss Bell herself, kneeling as she peered beneath a water trough, the curls around her face nearly even with the floor.

"Come here, you wicked creature," she said in an amused voice. "You think you are quite clever, don't you, hiding under there?"

Roland could not resist. He approached quietly, clasping his hands behind his back. "Good morning, Miss Bell."

Miss Bell jolted, banging her head on the trough and letting out a sharp yelp.

"Blast." Roland hurried forward. He'd only meant to surprise her. "Are you all right?"

She squinted up at him, rubbing her head as she sat back on her heels. "I admit, I've been better."

Roland grimaced and crouched beside her. "I am sorry. Truly. May I look?" If she was bleeding . . .

Miss Bell shook her head. "I am fine, I promise."

She did seem fine. There was no sign of the unfocused vision or slurred language that afflicted many of his friends after a bout of boxing. On the contrary, her eyes were bright and purposeful, and her words held all of the spirit he'd come to expect from her.

She smelled sweet, like cherries.

He hastily stood and held out his hand to her. "Might I be of assistance, Miss Bell? Are you looking for something?"

"No, I simply enjoy exploring dusty old stables," she said wryly as she took his hand.

His cheek twitched. "Then you are in luck. Mine is the oldest and dustiest in the county."

Her eyebrows shot upwards, and before she could say anything, he pulled her to her feet. It wasn't difficult, as Miss Bell was as slender as she was unexpected.

As soon as she found her feet, she took back her hand and stepped away. "I am sorry, I should not have said that about your stables. I'm certain they are well cared for."

"I am far from offended, I assure you," he said, crossing his arms. "But I am curious what you were doing just now."

She blew out a breath and gestured at the trough. "I am attempting to fix the rift I created between myself and your mother."

He squinted. "I am afraid I cannot see the connection between my mother and crawling about the stables."

"She has lost her cat," she said. "I am hoping if I am able to return it . . ."

Understanding dawned. "She'll forget your mistake of last evening?"

"Precisely."

Roland crouched once again and peered beneath the trough. Two yellow eyes stared back at him. "It is an admirable plan," he said. "My mother loves that cat like a second child." Never mind that it was a wretchedly spoiled creature that hissed at Roland whenever Mother was not present.

Miss Bell knelt beside him. "If only I had a treat to bribe him with."

"Perhaps a few of your sister's comfits," he said with a grin.

Miss Bell looked up at him sharply. "What?"

"Comfits?" he repeated, one brow raised. "Your sister Cassandra had a great deal of them in her trunk."

"Oh. Right. She mentioned that little mix-up." Miss Bell cleared her throat. "Yes, Cassie is very fond of sweets, but I daresay a cat would be more motivated by a bit of milk or meat. Having none on hand . . ."

She knelt on the stable floor once more, balancing on her elbows.

"Come here, you pretty thing," she said softly, holding out one hand. "Come out and I will take you to the house for some cream."

The yellow eyes tipped to one side, as if the cat was considering the proposition.

45

"I won't hurt you, I promise." Miss Bell slid her hand closer. "Come on now, be a dear."

Roland sat back on his heels, watching the young lady before him in bewilderment. Everything he had heard about Miss Bell—and had experienced briefly for himself in London when they'd met—told him she was refined and sophisticated. And yet there she was, practically lying in the dirt, talking to a cat.

As he watched, the cat crept forward and licked Miss Bell's extended hand. "That's it, come out," she encouraged it as she slowly drew backwards. The cat followed, stepping into the light—and revealing its gray coat of fur from nose to tail.

Roland coughed. "Miss Bell, I do believe we have a problem."

"A problem?" She was beaming, stroking the cat's arched back as it purred.

"That is not my mother's cat."

She jerked her head up to stare at him. "Pardon?"

He could not help a short laugh. "My mother's cat, Sir Chester, is black and white, and much more ill-tempered. In fact, you might consider yourself lucky not to have found him."

"Not her cat." Miss Bell turned her eyes back to the cat, now rubbing against her skirts. "Thunder and turf. Though I cannot say I am surprised, considering my unfortunate luck lately." She sighed and continued to pet the smooth gray fur.

"Unfortunate luck?" Roland asked. "How do you mean?" If anything, *he* was the one with bad luck, returning home to his mother's ambush of a house party.

46

"Well, first Vi—" She stopped, then gulped. "That is, first Cassie grew sick. And then, of course, the incident with your mother's painting. Now I bungle the one thing that might have redeemed me."

Roland eyed Miss Bell. She focused on the cat, but her back was stiff. Was it worry for her sister? "Might I ask after your sister's health? Will she be joining us today?"

She shook her head. "No, I'm afraid she will need to recover for a few days at the least."

"I am sorry to hear it." He leaned forward conspiratorially. "Though I admit I was intimidated at the prospect of telling the two of you apart."

Miss Bell continued petting the cat, but her eyes took on a new wariness. "I do not think it would be very difficult. C-Cassie and I are quite different in personality, if not in looks."

Roland clasped his hands behind his back. "Really? I spoke with her only briefly when you both first arrived, but it seemed you both at least share the inclination to speak your minds."

"Oh." Miss Bell gulped and looked down. "I must assure you I do not normally act like this. I'm afraid I've been a bit out of sorts with Cassie being ill, and then with that . . . misunderstanding after dinner last night."

"A misunderstanding with my mother would unhinge nearly anyone," he said as way of reassurance, though he was not sure why he needed to reassure her. Did she think speaking her mind was a negative quality in a woman? He had never thought so, considering he'd had his mother as his example growing up. Mother had a different way of expressing herself—more crafty than outspoken—but she never failed to make clear how she felt about something.

Miss Bell picked up the cat and stood. "I had better go inside and continue the search. Likely Miss Tindale has already found the real Sir Chester."

"Which would be a terrible thing?"

"I suppose not. But I am a bit more desperate for your mother's approval than Miss Tindale."

He nearly asked her why, but he caught himself. A delicate balance existed at this house party. He was certain all the guests knew why they'd been invited—to see if one of the young ladies could tempt him into a proposal. But they couldn't very well talk about it as if it were common knowledge.

Miss Bell sighed and held out the cat to him. He stared at the creature, then at her. "Er, it isn't mine."

"I know," she said with a furrowed brow. "I just thought perhaps you knew who it belonged to."

"The stables, I imagine." He took a step back. He'd been around his mother's cat enough times to be wary of sharp claws. "To keep the vermin out."

"Oh." She brought the cat back into her arms and tipped her head up at him. "You aren't frightened of it, are you?"

"If you knew Sir Chester, you would understand my hesitation," he said.

"Not all cats are horrible." She gave the cat in her arms one last pat before setting him on the ground. "This one is rather sweet, I think."

The cat scampered away, though it paused at the stable

doors and looked back, as if to ensure they both watched it still. Then it disappeared out into the cold.

"Might I accompany you up to the house?" Roland asked. They were going the same way, after all. But even if they hadn't, he felt the strangest urge to prolong this conversation with Miss Bell. When they'd met in London, he'd known only the barest details of her, a hurried sketch of her character. Now it was as though each time he spoke to her, that sketch became more detailed, with small spots of watercolor slipping in around her.

He was far too pragmatic to lose his heart on a whim. But if this small bit of intrigue he felt towards Miss Bell meant anything . . . he wanted to see where it led.

"Of course," Miss Bell said. Then she looked down at herself and winced. "If you can bear to be seen with me, that is."

Her flowered dress was covered in dirt, and she brushed at her skirts. A few of her golden curls had escaped her coiffure and lay limply against her neck. Though a lovely neck it was, he could not help but observe.

"I think I can manage," he said, offering his arm. Miss Bell hesitated, her gaze flicking up to his. Then she slipped her hand around the crook of his elbow, her touch light.

He led her from the stables and back towards the house, attempting to keep up their easy conversation. He pointed out details of the manor and estate she might find interesting—the addition to the east wing his father had built a decade ago, and the best place to find wild strawberries in the summer. Miss Bell nodded and replied as was appropriate. Too appropriate, really. Was this an attempt to prove him wrong, that she did *not* speak her mind?

Women were odd creatures indeed.

Upon entering the house, Miss Bell drew her hand from his arm. "Thank you for seeing me back, Mr. Hastings."

"Well, it would have been a great deal more awkward if I'd simply followed you here."

A flash in her blue eyes. Amusement. But she turned away before he saw her smile.

"Roland, there you are."

Mother marched across the entry, and in her arms was the long-haired black-and-white cat. Miss Tindale trailed behind, hands clasped neatly in front of her.

"I see you've found Sir Chester," Roland said. At least he wouldn't be forced to join the search.

"Yes, no thanks to you." Mother frowned at him deeply. Roland knew better than to think she was irritated he hadn't helped look for the cat. No, she was put out because he'd skipped breakfast. "Fortunately, Miss Tindale was untiring in her efforts and located him upstairs."

"I could hardly let the poor creature go missing, not when it distressed you so, Mrs. Hastings." Miss Tindale peered up at Roland through her lashes. "It was the least I could do."

"Your actions are much appreciated," Mother said, stroking Sir Chester's back. "How glad I am to have such a thoughtful and kind guest in my home."

She did not look at Miss Bell as she spoke, but the

slight was obvious all the same. Roland groaned inwardly. Mother and her pride. Miss Bell was their guest just as much as Miss Tindale, no matter the incident last night.

"Yes, thank you, Miss Tindale," Roland said. "And Miss Bell, as well. I found her in the stables, intent on her own search for the cat."

"That is why I am so dirty," Miss Bell added quickly. "I was sorry to hear he was missing and wished to help."

"I see." Mother scrutinized Miss Bell. "In any case, Miss Tindale asked for a tour of the house, and I cannot refuse her in anything since she found my Chester. Roland, would you join us?"

He forced a smile. He did not truly have a choice. "Of course."

Mother turned to Miss Bell. "I am certain you will wish to change, or of course you would be welcome as well." She sounded as welcoming as a bear in its den.

"Yes, indeed," Miss Bell said with a too-bright smile. "Perhaps later."

She curtsied and hurried up the stairs. Miss Tindale immediately claimed his side and began questioning him on the stained-glass window in the library, but his attention stayed on Miss Bell—her bouncing curls and slim shoulders—until her skirts whisked around the upstairs corner.

She did not look back, a disappointment Roland had not thought to expect.

CHAPTER 7

THE NEXT TWO days passed in an exhausting tumble. Cassie had to take care every second of every day to watch her mouth, her reactions, her very thoughts. She still gave a little jolt whenever someone called her Miss Bell rather than Miss Cassandra—never more so than when Mr. Hastings did it—but her caution began to pay off. She made no more horribly egregious errors.

Though she could not deny the warmth in her stomach each time Mr. Hastings looked at her. But it was hardly her fault that her sister's intended was unfairly handsome.

Which was an entirely new sort of problem. When Mr. Hastings had found her in the stables, she'd been caught off guard and, as in all their interactions before, acted too much like herself. He now thought Vivian was *outspoken*, for heaven's sake. That had prompted her careful reevaluation of strategy. She managed the situation instead of attempting to lead it. She stayed with Mr. Hastings and

Miss Tindale, offering only the blandest and safest opinions during their conversations. At the very least, she could ensure the other two were not on their own overmuch.

"I am sorry I cannot do more," Cassie told Vivian as she dressed for dinner four days after arriving at Hartfield Court. "But I assure you it's for the best. Once you are entirely well, you can charm everyone."

"If I can ever recover," Vivian muttered from the bed. She had only just begun to look a bit like her own self, not running to the chamber pot every hour. But her illness left her weak and frail. When she tried to stand, her legs shook and she nearly fainted.

"You will," Cassie reassured her, pulling on her elbow-length gloves. "Dr. Duttle said three more days at the soonest, though, and as much as I wish to relinquish my role as Vivian Bell, I'll not do it at the cost of your health. You must be patient."

"I know," Vivian said with a sigh. "And I am not ungrateful. I know you have done all you can."

"You know I would do anything for you, but I shall be glad when this is over." When Vivian could take her rightful place at Mr. Hastings's side and Cassie could return home to Grandpapa and her quiet life.

She looked at her reflection in the mirror. She wore Vivian's vivid red dress, an unusual color for young ladies, who were expected to stay within the realms of pastels. Cassie would never have chosen for herself, but she admitted she looked rather well in it, with her hair swept up to the crown of her head and embellished with a bit of holly she'd found on a walk that morning, which added a bit of Christmas festivity to her look. She wondered if Mr. Hastings liked holly . . .

Cassie tore her eyes from the mirror.

"Enjoy your dinner," Vivian said, a note of sadness in her voice.

Cassie took a deep breath and turned to face her sister. This house party was all Vivian had dreamed of for weeks, and now she was missing it. The least Cassie could do was keep her thoughts from Mr. Hastings and focus on her sister. "Would you like me to send up a tray? Or just more tea?"

Vivian made a face. "I'm afraid nothing sounds particularly appetizing at the moment."

"Tea it is." Cassie forced a smile. "I will see you after, I promise. I'm certain I'll be able to avoid disaster again."

"Shall we have some music?" Mrs. Hastings called out as the party settled into the drawing room after dinner. "We've hardly had time in the last two days, but I would so enjoy hearing the young ladies sing."

"Of course. That is a splendid idea," Miss Tindale said as Miss Marsden nodded her agreement. "I have just the song in mind."

Unsurprising. She likely had a hundred songs prepared for a moment such as this. But Cassie had no time for petty thoughts. Because Mrs. Hastings's attention then turned to her. In nearly four days of pretending to be Vivian, Cassie had not thought to anticipate *this*.

"Oh, no, I couldn't tonight," she stammered. Why?

Why couldn't she tonight? Her mind scurried to find a plausible reason. "I haven't practiced?" she finally said, more of a question than she wanted it to be.

"A true artist can create under any circumstances." Mrs. Hastings fixed her with a stare, as if daring Cassie to argue.

"Perhaps I might only play instead of sing." That would be feasible. She could manage a quick little tune.

"Nonsense. I hear you have an excellent voice, and I should like the opportunity to judge for myself," Mrs. Hastings said briskly.

Cassie forced a little cough. "Truly, I think I might have a sore throat. Perhaps another night—"

"I'll not take no for an answer, Miss Bell." Mrs. Hastings narrowed her eyes. "I insist."

Cassie opened her mouth to refuse, then stopped. *Vivian* would never refuse. So she shut her mouth and managed a weak nod. Thankfully Miss Tindale offered to play first, which allowed Cassie time to assess her options.

The problem lay much deeper than possessing an inadequate singing voice. Really, Cassie could sing well enough—alone. But whenever Cassie attempted to perform in front of anyone other than her immediate family, her voice . . . well, her voice squeaked. Badly. So badly, in fact, that the last time her mother insisted she sing in front of company—two years ago—her dim-sighted great-aunt Wilmington had insisted there was a mouse beneath her chair.

But when Vivian was known for having a lovely voice, what was Cassie to do?

Miss Tindale began playing her piece, a sweet folk

song, her full, steady voice joining the tones of the pianoforte after a few measures. Cassie was sitting stiffly, hands clutched together in her lap, when Mr. Hastings caught her eye. He furrowed his brow and mouthed a few words at her. But since Cassie was as terrible at reading lips as she was at performing, his message of "Tar ewe all night" was not particularly reassuring.

Cassie shook her head slightly, hoping Mr. Hastings would understand that she had no idea what he was saying. Then she looked again at Miss Tindale—composed, effortless Miss Tindale—and tried to think of a plan. Perhaps she might pretend to faint. But then she would be relegated to her bed like Vivian, which would defeat the entire purpose of this charade. The same was true of persisting with her lie about a sore throat.

Her only choice was to perform—and hope with every bone in her body that her voice was no longer frightened of people.

Miss Tindale finished her song to great applause, and Miss Marsden began her performance, her light and airy voice barely audible above the pianoforte. Cassie's heart thumped faster and faster, nearly leaping into her throat when Miss Marsden curtsied and moved back to her chair.

"Miss Bell," Mrs. Hastings said, nodding to where the instrument stood beside the wide, dark windows.

Cassie somehow managed to seat herself before the pianoforte and rested her fingers on the keys. She'd chosen her song, "Whilst Shepherds Watched Their Flocks by Night," very carefully. First of all, it was a song she could recall by memory, as she hadn't brought her music to Hartfield Court. And secondly, she hoped playing a familiar carol would soften Mrs. Hastings's opinion of her. This *was* a Christmas party, after all.

Cassie glanced up for a brief moment, spotting Mr. Hastings at the back of the chairs. He had stood sometime during the other performances and now crossed his arms, eyeing her in an unnerving way.

She pressed her fingers down into a chord, played a few measures, trying to breathe deeply. At least her fingers remembered the notes well enough. Then there was nothing for it but to start singing.

"Whilst Shepherds wa-atched their flocks by night." The first line went fairly smooth, though her voice cracked slightly on a high note. She went on. *"All seated on the ground."*

That wasn't bad, really. Her voice was not nearly as confident as Miss Tindale's, but neither was anyone covering their ears. She started into the next line.

"The Angel of the Lord came down and glory shone all round." Perhaps she could do this. Survive, that was. Another few stanzas and she could retreat to her chair.

"Fear not, said he—" Her voice jumped, leaping into a squeak that would have made dogs howl. She paused, swallowing hard, then continued. *"Fear not, said he for mighty dread—"* Another squeak, higher and louder. Cassie's eyes flew up to her watching audience. Miss Tindale hid a smile behind her fan, Miss Marsden's eyes were wide, and Mrs. Hastings watched with frightening interest. Then Cassie locked gazes with Mr. Hastings for the briefest of moments. He straightened, alarmed, no doubt, by the blazing panic on her face.

But all she could do was finish the song.

"For mighty dread had seized their troubled mi—" The sound that next escaped her mouth would have put a dying animal to shame. Cassie slammed her mouth shut, her hands frozen over the keys. What was worse, fleeing in embarrassment or continuing to sing in embarrassment?

A crash sounded across the room. Someone gasped as the entire party turned in their chairs, and Cassie stood abruptly, the stool skittering away from her knees.

"Blast." Mr. Hastings put his hands to his waist, looking down at the floor near his feet, where shattered pieces of ceramic lay, some still spinning.

"Roland." Mrs. Hastings stood, her face aghast. "My vase."

"I am sorry, Mother. It was an accident." He sounded truly apologetic. "I know you liked it."

Mrs. Hastings pursed her lips, as if holding back a scolding. "No matter," she finally managed, then called for servants to clean up the mess.

Mr. Hastings turned to Cassie and—he winked. *Winked.*

Had he done it on purpose? To save her?

The party settled back in their chairs, and Cassie cleared her throat. "Perhaps I might finish another time. I find my nerves are a bit rattled."

"Of course, dear," the matronly Mrs. Marsden assured her, and Cassie hurried back to her seat. Safe. For now, at least.

Mrs. Hastings still did not look particularly happy about the way the evening had gone, especially as the guests broke into groups for cards and conversation. It would be best for Cassie to avoid her the rest of the night. In fact, it would likely be best to avoid everyone for the remainder of the night.

When all eyes were occupied, she slipped from the drawing room, grateful the door's hinges were far better oiled than her voice. The cool quiet welcomed her, and she inhaled a long breath. She couldn't go upstairs yet; Vivian would be full of questions as to why she was so early in coming to bed. So Cassie retreated down the corridor until she found a rounded alcove lined with windows. She sat on the ledge and leaned against the glass, closing her eyes.

But laughter echoed down the corridor, invading her quiet. Cassie peered around the corner. A figure stood outside the drawing room, shutting the door behind him. Broad shoulders and a mess of dark hair. Mr. Hastings.

She shrank back into her alcove. Perhaps he would go upstairs and bypass her altogether. But his footsteps came closer until he rounded the corner and spotted her.

"There you are." He stopped a few paces away, his eyes flickering in the candlelight. "I wanted to see that you were all right."

His kindness tugged at her heart. He was concerned —for her.

She forced a smile. "Yes, perfectly all right. Better now that I do not have to sing."

He stepped forward, crossing his arms. "Are you certain? I am sorry my mother pressed you so. If you *do* have a sore throat—"

Cassie shook her head fervently. "Oh, I'm not ill, I

assure you. It must be . . . it must be this cold weather affecting my voice."

He nodded, a small smile pulling up the corners of his mouth, but he allowed her very obvious falsehood to stand. He glanced out the window behind her. "I daresay it will snow soon, which would delight Mother."

"I did not take your mother for an enthusiast of snow." Cassie wasn't particularly fond of the stuff herself. It was lovely, she supposed, but she did not relish the feel of it melting in her boots.

Mr. Hastings gave a short laugh. "I would not word it that way. She thinks snow is unfailingly romantic, and that it will surely make me fall in love at last."

Cassie blinked. What was she to say to that? Perhaps a change in subject was best. "Thank you." The words nearly burst from her.

He raised an eyebrow. "Thank you?"

"For earlier," she said quickly. "For distracting everyone with the vase so I did not need to finish my song."

"Oh, that." He sat on the window ledge across the alcove from her. He was not particularly close, but Cassie's pulse ticked faster. "I'm afraid I cannot claim credit for rescuing you. I was born clumsy, you see."

Cassie's lips curved upward. "And you somehow happened to shatter a vase halfway across the room?"

"It's a dreadful curse," he said with a grin.

"Well, I shall thank you all the same, especially since your mother seemed most upset at the loss."

He waved that off. "She'll be glad for it when we go to London again and she has a reason to shop for another."

"You'll attend the Season, then?" Why did that thought make London suddenly more appealing?

Mr. Hastings shrugged. "If I must."

She wanted to press him further, ask why he seemed reluctant to go. Because it looked as if they had that very much in common. But Vivian *adored* London, so it would not make sense for Cassie to suddenly have developed a dislike for it. She sighed. This pretense was getting more and more difficult by the day.

"Why the sigh?" he asked, leaning forward.

"Nothing," she said hastily. What would he say if he knew her true thoughts? That she was ruminating over the unexpected difficulties of convincing him that she was her sister?

He narrowed his eyes as if he meant to press her. She scrambled for something else to say. "That is, I admit I am missing home, and my family. I've never spent Christmas away before."

"But you have your sister, at least."

"Yes, of course. But I shall miss my grandfather especially."

He nodded. "You said you are close to him."

He remembered that? She'd mentioned it days ago.

"Yes," she said, tugging up her gloves. "He always makes Christmas special. The song I played is a favorite of his, and he insists I play it every year."

Mr. Hastings smiled. "My father loved Christmas as well. We often hosted a dinner on Christmas Day, and Father enjoyed having his friends and family around him." His smile faded. "You said the other day that your grand-father's parrot made him feel young again, helped him relive his favorite memories. I think Christmas did that for my father."

Cassie wrapped her arms around herself. Sitting by the chill window sent bumps along her exposed skin, but she hardly noticed as she tried to remember what she knew of the Hastings family. When had the elder Mr. Hastings died?

"Your father . . ." she began, uncertain how to phrase her question.

"He died a year ago, before Christmas." Mr. Hastings leaned forward to place his elbows on his knees. "It makes this time of year difficult, especially for my mother." He swallowed. "Though I also miss him, of course."

She hardly knew what to say to that. She bit her lip, ready to make an attempt, but thankfully he spoke before she could say something horribly inadequate.

"This house party has been good for my mother, though," he said. "She takes a strange amount of joy from planning menus and activities."

"What does your mother have planned for tomorrow?" she asked. "I feel I ought to be prepared, for obvious reasons."

Mr. Hastings grinned, and the unexpected seriousness of their conversation lifted. "I'm sorry to say I haven't the faintest. I find it better to leave the planning to her, because she does everything how she wishes no matter what I say. Saves me a great deal of time and effort."

"If you had your say, what would we be doing?"

"We wouldn't be having this house party, to start."

She blinked. "Oh."

He grimaced. "I am sorry, I did not mean it like that.

I've enjoyed the past few days, for the most part. But I will admit I had no hand in organizing this party, as I had no idea of its existence until the day I arrived from London."

Was that why he had been in a bad humor that day when their trunks had been switched? But then she could hardly blame him. She hadn't wanted to come either, after all. She almost said that aloud but again stopped herself. Because *Vivian* had wanted to come.

"Then besides the preferable option of there being no house party at all," she said lightly, "what activity would you choose for tomorrow? Because if the host does not enjoy himself, I cannot think why a house party would be worth the effort."

He laughed. "You and my mother have very different views on house parties." He seemed to consider the question more seriously, rubbing his chin. "Anything outdoors, I suppose. I cannot stand to be cooped up, even when it is cold." He paused. "Perhaps archery."

"Are you good at it?"

"If you had asked me as a youth, I would have boasted endlessly about my prowess with a bow. But now I cannot say I've touched one in years. I cannot seem to find the time."

"That sounds like a problem to be rectified," she said firmly. "We have the time now, after all."

He leaned back against the window. "You underestimate my mother's abilities. You've seen how good she is at filling all seconds of the day."

"True enough." But she could not help but think that if he was forced to attend every event, he might as well enjoy one of them.

Voices echoed down the corridor as the drawing room opened once again. "Roland?" Mrs. Hastings called.

Roland—Mr. Hastings, that was—raised a finger to his lips and grinned. Cassie held her breath. She wanted to be caught in a compromising situation even less than he did. Although perhaps that was *one* way for Vivian to achieve her marriage goals.

Footsteps moved towards them, and the two of them dared not move. Cassie's eyes went to his, as if pulled by a current. He stared back at her, the amusement in his expression shifting to something . . . different.

"Roland?" Mrs. Hastings called again, a sharp edge to her voice.

But Roland did not move. That is, his body did not. His eyes, however, wandered her face, slowly, curiously. And she found she could not look away.

Mrs. Hasting's footsteps moved, back inside the drawing room. When the door shut behind her, it snapped the pull between them, and Cassie drew herself backward, bracing her hands on either side of the window ledge. What had *that* been?

Roland cleared his throat. "I am sorry for making you hide. But I thought we both needed a respite from my mother."

"You are not wrong," she murmured, still attempting to collect her thoughts. She'd never felt . . . felt . . . *whatever* that had been between them. She looked back up at him, as if to test herself, to see if it would happen again. He offered a slight smile, and although her stomach warmed slightly, she did not wish to fling herself into his arms like she had only moments before.

It was his fault, she decided, for being so kind and good-looking. Why, he likely had ladies flinging themselves at him with every flash of his smile. She only needed to be on her guard, that was all. At least with the two of them together out here, she was assured Miss Tindale was most certainly *not* with him.

"So tell me," Roland said, as if his mother had not just nearly caught them together, "what activity would you choose for tomorrow, if you could?"

"I hardly know," she said. "I'm afraid I'm not quite as fond of the outdoors as you."

"Still," he said. "If you had all of tomorrow to yourself, what would you do?"

Cassie knew what Vivian would want to do—pay visits, shop, attend parties and dinners. But for once she wanted to give an honest answer. "First, I would sleep far too late into the morning. Then I would eat my fill of pastries and chocolate, perhaps read a book or spend time with my sister. And then I would go in search of that little gray cat in the stables."

"The cat?"

"Yes," she said. "After the stress I caused it the other day, I daresay it deserves a treat."

Roland stayed quiet a moment. "I think that sounds like a wonderful day," he finally said.

And Cassie couldn't help thinking the only thing that might improve it was if he was there too.

CHAPTER 8

WHEN CASSIE WOKE the next morning, it was with a smile.

She sat up in bed and stretched. Her curtains were still drawn, but dim light shown about the edges. She padded to the window and parted the curtains, looking out at the gray skies and light mist of rain that coated the glass.

And yet still Cassie smiled.

She should be exhausted. She couldn't say how late she and Roland had stayed in that alcove the evening before—had the clock struck one o'clock, or perhaps two? The other guests had eventually made their way upstairs and gone to bed. But not the two of them, tucked away in their peaceful seclusion. They'd talked and laughed—quietly—long into the night.

They'd talked of everything. Cassie had shared amusing stories from growing up a twin, and Roland told her more of his Christmas memories with his father. Their topics ranged from literature to opera, with time allotted for the latest scandal about the prince regent and the tendency of Roland's butler to cough precisely three times upon entering a room.

They'd talked so much that Cassie had forgotten to be on her guard.

Her smile faded, and she let the curtain fall back into place. She thought over all she'd said last night—or at least she tried to. They'd spent hours together, but it had felt more like minutes. Had she said anything to give away her true identity? Likely small things here and there. But he wouldn't really remember all that anyway. Would he?

A knock came at the door, and Cassie went to answer it, throwing her dressing gown around her shoulders.

"Vivian," she scolded upon seeing her sister leaning heavily on the doorframe. "What are you doing out of bed?"

"You didn't come to see me last night," she said in a weak voice. "I was worried."

"I was tired, that was all." Cassie ushered her inside. "Come sit down before Dr. Dutton sentences you to longer in bed."

Vivian lowered herself to an armchair. "How was dinner last night?"

"Well, I was forced to sing, so I'll let you imagine the rest."

Vivian's eyes widened. "You sang?"

"No, I croaked, but luckily my song came to a sudden end."

She shook her head. "Heavens, Cassie, sometimes I cannot decide if this deception is worth all this trouble."

"That certainly makes two of us," Cassie said dryly. "Though I've thought so from the beginning."

"It's no use changing course now," Vivian said with a frown. "I shall have a mountain of things to fix when we switch back, but that should be soon enough. I feel much better today."

"You can barely stand," Cassie pointed out. "The doctor said at least two more days."

"Soon enough," Vivian repeated, rubbing her forehead. "And what of Mr. Hastings? Did you talk with him last night?"

Cassie coughed. "Yes, of course. That is my job, after all. Distracting him."

"And what did you talk of?"

Everything and nothing. The grandest ideas and the silliest details.

But she could not tell Vivian all that. And she especially could not tell her about the way Roland had looked at her last night.

"Opera came up, I believe," she managed instead.

"That seems safe enough." Vivian frowned. "Though I hope you did not give him the impression I liked them overmuch."

"I would never," Cassie said with a laugh. "I've entirely ruined your singing reputation, but your opinions of opera are intact, I assure you."

"Good," Vivian said. "Less work for me." She stood carefully. "I am going to lie down, but please come see me later. I am dreadfully bored."

Poor Vivian, shut away at a house party with nothing to do but rest and read the books Jennings had brought her from the scarce library. "Of course," Cassie said. "You know I will."

Vivian left, and Cassie dressed quickly, pinning her hair up carefully. Far more carefully than she had in the past. She could hardly look unpresentable, though, could she?

Another knock at her door. Was it Vivian again? "Come in," she called, tugging at a curl in the mirror.

A maid opened the door, balancing a tray against her hip. "Pardon me, Miss Bell, but I was sent with a tray for you."

"For me?" Cassie turned on her chair. "You do not mean my sister, Miss Cassandra, who is ill?" Surely this tray was meant for Vivian.

"No, miss, for you." The maid set the tray on the little table before the fireplace. "Mr. Hastings himself asked it to be sent."

Cassie went to the table. The tray was near to bursting with a variety of pastries and a steaming cup of chocolate. Her mouth dropped. He'd remembered.

"Thank you," she said to the maid, who curtsied and departed. Cassie sat at the table and took a sip of the chocolate, the sharp bitterness and warmth mixing delightfully together.

He'd remembered.

Such a small thing shouldn't bring her so much pleasure, but it did. Cassie often felt forgotten behind her sister, which she truly did not mind. She loved Vivian and would never blame her for it.

But to be seen like Roland saw her . . .

She straightened. No. He did not see her as Cassie. He saw her as the perfectly proper Miss Vivian Bell, save with a few quirks Cassie had unwittingly added. She could not allow herself to begin to think he cared for her. That would only lead to pain.

But she still had to continue on this path until Vivian recovered. She simply needed to sort her feelings better. Roland could be nothing more than a friend, her future brother-in-law.

She picked up a pastry filled with red jam and took a small bite. It was delicious, of course. And quite suddenly, despite her confusion and trepidation over the entire affair, she wanted to repay Roland's kindness. He gave so much of himself, to his mother and his guests and now to her, that he deserved some happiness all his own.

But what? He'd mentioned archery the night before, but even now as she looked out the window, large drops of water began hitting the diamond-paned glass. They could hardly shoot outside in this weather. How else might she surprise him, as he had surprised her with breakfast?

An idea took root in Cassie's mind, then began to blossom and unfurl. She grinned. Perfect.

Roland looked again at the note in his hand as he slipped down the back stairwell. *Ballroom at one o'clock*, it said, with no name or any clue as to its writer. He'd studied it a hundred times since finding it slipped under his door when he'd returned from his morning ride, and he'd also studied each of the young women when the party had gathered to play cards after breakfast. Miss Tindale had acted her usual proper and insightful self, Miss Marsden had hardly peeped out a word in his presence, and Miss Bell...

Well, he knew who he hoped had sent the note. Because he hadn't been able to keep his eyes from Miss Bell all morning—the graceful curve of her neck, her fair curls bouncing as she laughed.

And from the many times he'd met her eyes, it seemed she wanted to look at him as well. The hours they'd spent together the night before, talking and laughing in the secluded alcove, had danced through his mind since they'd parted. He'd hardly slept for thinking of it, for thinking of *her*. He tried to force his hopefulness away; a few conversations did not a love match make. Even if they had been wonderful conversations. Even if he'd never spoken so freely with another person since his father had died.

Roland drew in a deep breath as he approached the ballroom, stuffing the note inside his jacket pocket. Thankfully, the ballroom was quite out of the way, or he would not risk meeting whoever had sent the note. But still, he looked up and down the corridor to ensure he was alone before stepping inside. Dim light seeped through the windows, the sun hidden behind the clouds and falling rain. He closed the door behind him. Was he here first?

"You are late," said a teasing voice.

He turned to see Miss Bell crossing the room, hands clasped behind her back as she moved toward him, dressed in a simple blue day dress. Even with the muted light around them, her eyes shone with a brightness that made his heart lighter.

Roland grinned. "I think being late is well within my rights, when I hadn't the faintest idea who extended such a mysterious invitation."

"Ah, but the mystery made it more exciting, did it not?" She stopped a few paces from him, her lips curving upwards.

"True enough." He crossed his arms. "Though perhaps your reason for inviting me was intrigue enough."

Her expression turned earnest. "Not so very intriguing, no. I only wanted to thank you for your thoughtfulness in sending me breakfast. It was very kind of you, and I was surprised you remembered, considering."

"Considering we spoke for nearly five hours last night?" He spoke quietly, as if they stood amidst a packed ballroom and not the empty one now surrounding them. "I find it hard to forget anything you say, Miss Bell."

She looked down, looping one arm behind her back to grasp her other elbow. "I . . . I enjoyed our conversation," she said.

"As did I." Roland could have said a great deal more, but there was no need to rush anything. If there *was* something between the two of them, they had time enough to discover the truth of it. The house party was only half over.

Miss Bell cleared her throat. "Anyway, I did not entice you here simply to thank you. I also wished to offer a surprise of my own."

He tilted his head, narrowing his eyes in false suspicion. "And what is that?"

"I wanted to give you the activity you wished for last

night, but since it is raining . . ." She waved a hand to the far end of the ballroom.

Roland turned. Across the room, below one of the chandeliers, stood an archery target—one he recognized immediately, even if he hadn't seen it in over a year. His mouth dropped as he stared.

"I managed to bribe a footman to set it all up," Miss Bell said quickly. "The room isn't very long, so I doubt the distance will be much of a challenge for you. And the footman wasn't entirely certain which equipment was yours, so he brought the lot of it."

Roland let out a soft laugh. "You've set up an archery range? Here in the ballroom."

Miss Bell swallowed. "I'm sorry, that was terribly forward of me, wasn't it? I should have asked permission instead of—"

He stepped forward and took her hand, lifting it between them. She stopped, her eyes focused on their joined hands.

"No, you should not have asked permission," he said. "That would have defeated the purpose of a surprise, would it not?"

She raised her gaze to meet his. "I . . . yes, quite right."

With her small, warm hand in his and her vivid blue eyes staring up at him, Roland's pulse leaped within him. He wanted to tell her this was the kindest thing anyone had ever done for him. But something in her wide eyes held him back.

"Good," he managed instead, reluctantly releasing her hand and stepping back. "Now, you ought to prepare yourself to be dazzled. I cannot be held responsible for any swooning once you witness my skill in archery firsthand."

Miss Bell laughed, a bit breathlessly. "I shall try to restrain myself."

They moved to the opposite wall from the target, where a long table had been laid with bows and arrows. Roland shot Miss Bell a sidelong glance as they walked. She absently rubbed the palm of her hand—the hand Roland had been holding not moments before. He allowed himself a small grin.

"I hope you have everything you need," she said as they reached the table. "I cannot say I am a great expert in the essentials of archery."

"So your skills are limited to critiquing art and taming cats." He moved to the bows, finding his favorite and gripping the handle. "I shall need to remember that."

"Why is that?"

He raised his eyebrow mischievously. "To remind myself you are not perfect."

She let out a sound crossed between a snort and a guffaw. "I think I provide you with reminders enough."

She had no idea how much her "reminders" charmed him. What she saw as embarrassing mistakes, he viewed as endearing eccentricities.

He set his bow down and picked up his stout leather brace, slipping it over his left arm and buckling it.

"I am sorry I do not have a brace or glove for you," he said as he next pulled on his shooting glove, a three-fingered contraption that buttoned at the wrist.

Miss Bell watched his motions with interest. "Oh, no matter. I had not intended to join you, only observe."

"We will see about that." Roland flexed his gloved hand. It had been so long. Would he even be able to properly string his bow?

"You do not want me to handle any sort of weapon, I assure you," she responded. "Someone would likely lose a finger."

He laughed. "I would be much more likely to lose a finger persuading a stubborn cat from beneath a trough."

"We each have our strengths, then." She nodded at his bow. "Come, Robin Hood, let me see this ability you've so boasted."

Roland took up his bow again, feeling the weight of the smooth, cool wood, nearly as tall as Miss Bell. He grasped the free end of the string and placed the bow in position, his right hand on the center of the handle, the bottom of the bow placed on the ground against his foot. In one swift movement born from years of practice, he pulled at the handle—the bow bending as it braced against his foot—and quickly slipped the eye of the string over the nock.

"That looked difficult," Miss Bell observed, stepping closer to examine his handiwork.

He laughed. "As I was trying to make it look effortless, I must count it a failure."

She grinned. "I was only attempting to save my true amazement for the actual shooting."

"Then ready yourself, madam," he said in as charismatic a voice as he could manage, taking an arrow from the table and stepping away. "For you shall not be disappointed."

Roland tested the strength of the string, and, finding it

sound, nocked the arrow to the string and raised the bow. Drawing the arrow back to his ear, he squinted one eye. He held his position another few seconds, making small adjustments in his form and aim, then released the arrow.

It flew across the ballroom and hit the target with a dull thunk on the outer white circle. He'd barely managed to hit the target.

"Well," came Miss Bell's amused voice from behind him as he lowered his bow. "If I cannot trust your word that you are an accomplished marksman, what can I trust?"

"The first shot hardly counts. You must allow me some practice."

She leaned back against the edge of the table. "And how much practice do you require? One year? Two?"

"Your teasing will get you in trouble sooner or later." He walked back toward the table.

"So long as it is later, I do not mind overmuch," she said, crossing her arms with a playful tilt to her head.

He'd planned to take another arrow from the closer end of the table, but at her words, he could not resist a change in direction. He moved straight at her, slowly. Her eyes widened as he stopped before her. She did not move from her position, though she straightened.

"And if trouble finds you sooner?" he said in a low voice, placing one hand on the table beside her as he leaned in.

She barely breathed, her eyes fixed on his. "I daresay I can manage a little trouble."

Roland dipped his head closer to hers, their faces inches apart. Her mouth parted, and he forgot that he was teasing her back, that he did not actually mean to kiss her. He forgot all the cautions he had given himself and the reminders that he needn't rush anything. Because in that moment he wanted nothing more than to close the distance between them and claim those soft pink lips as his.

CHAPTER 9

CASSIE STARED UP AT ROLAND, her breath caught in her throat. She dared not move—giving any freedom to her limbs would surely result in her closing the gap between them and discovering what all the fuss with kissing was about.

His coffee-colored eyes flicked over her, and for a moment the teasing in his expression was replaced by a look she'd never seen on a man. At least, not on a man looking at *her*.

Then he flashed a grin and leaned closer. She inhaled a sharp breath, but he simply reached behind her, took an arrow from the table, and stepped away.

"Allow me ten shots, Miss Bell," he said, nocking the arrow on his bow. "You can resume your teasing if I haven't improved."

"You may count on it," Cassie somehow convinced her voice to say. She did not move from where she leaned on the table, not trusting her legs to support her weight.

It took him less than ten shots before he hit the gold

center circle. He did not crow in victory but sent her a sly smile and offered a bow as she applauded. They spent the next hour—or two or three, she couldn't tell by the light—talking as Roland reacquainted himself with his long-neglected archery skills. Just as last night, their conversation ran the gamut in terms of topics, and never was there an awkward moment between them. It was difficult to remember to be Vivian, to respond as she would. Talking with Roland was like stepping into a swift winter wind. It swept her away, twirled her about, and made her head feel light and dizzy.

And like a winter wind, she had no idea where she was headed.

Cassie pushed that thought away, concentrating again on Roland's laugh, his quick wit and dancing eyes. She simply wanted to enjoy the here and now.

When at last the light outside the windows began to fade slightly, Roland let out a sigh and lowered his bow. "I think that is the most escape we can hope for today. Mother is no doubt wondering where I am, full of lectures about neglecting my guests."

"*I* am a guest," Cassie pointed out. "So you needn't feel guilty."

He came back to the table and laid his bow down. "Believe me, guilt is the last emotion I am feeling at the moment." He said it lightly, but somehow his voice still carried a note of meaning. Cassie's heart quickened, and she ordered it to calm. He could have meant a million different things.

Roland crossed his arms. "But before we abandon our pleasant sojourn here, I must insist you take a turn."

"Those words will be etched on your gravestone," Cassie warned.

He fought a grin. "They will be well worth it if you are as bad as you say. Then at least you can provide the both of us with some entertainment."

"How can I refuse such an offer when it includes guaranteed mocking?"

"Oh, I do not guarantee it. That depends entirely on your lack of skill." He picked up a smaller bow. "Here, use this. It was mine when I was a boy, so it will be easier to draw."

"I suppose I could try," she said reluctantly as he strung the bow and gathered a small bundle of arrows for her. She didn't particularly want to make a fool of herself, but archery seemed to make him happy. And for reasons she was not very clear on, she wanted to make Roland happy.

"I have every faith in you." He held out the bow with a gleam of mischief in his eyes.

"All right." Cassie took the bow and the bundle of arrows. She moved closer to the target and set the arrows on the ground. He remained at the table, no doubt in fear for his life.

She had used a bow and arrow before but not often. Neither she nor Vivian had a special fondness for archery, so revealing her lack of skill was thankfully not adding to the deception. Cassie nocked an arrow on the string as she'd watched Roland do, then raised the bow. Drawing the arrow back to her ear, she stared down the length of the smooth wood and aimed at the center of the target.

She released the arrow, and off it flew. That is, until it skittered to the floor not twenty feet away.

"So it wasn't false modesty," Roland said from behind her, a laugh hiding in his voice.

Cassie gave an exaggerated huff. "I allowed you ten shots, so I expect the same courtesy."

He held up his hands. "Of course, of course. Unless you wish for my help?"

She'd been bending to fetch another arrow, but she nearly fell over as she spotted him approaching from the corner of her eye.

"No, no," she said hastily, finding her balance. "No, I will be perfectly fine on my own, thank you."

He gave her a strange look. "As you wish," he said, then returned to his spot near the table.

Cassie let out a breath of relief as she turned back to the target. Her heart was already a mess, her stomach made of twisting currents. Having him too near would wreak even more havoc on her body. It was best if he stood far, *far* away.

She raised the bow again, this time pulling back the string even farther. She didn't mind his teasing, not when he took hers so well, but she wanted to impress him all the same. *This* arrow would make it to the target. Aiming the tip of her arrow, she tried to keep her arms as steady as possible. She relaxed her right hand, preparing to release.

"Roland?"

Cassie's arm jerked at the voice. She yelped at the same moment that her arrow tore from her fingers—

—and buried itself in the polished wood of the open ballroom door, not inches from Mrs. Hastings's wide, white eyes.

"Heavens," the woman gasped, clutching a hand to her heart as she staggered back.

"Mrs. Hastings," Cassie squeaked, nearly dropping her bow.

Mrs. Hastings stared at her, then her eyes flew to the target on one end of the ballroom.

"Mother, are you all right?" Roland crossed the room, his brow dipped in concern.

Mrs. Hastings waved off her son, her eyes flashing dangerously. "What," she said, her tone sharp as a cat's claws, "is happening here?"

Cassie felt a mad desire to dash away, to open one of those wide windows and flee outside. But then, this had been her fault. She could hardly leave Roland here to face the consequences of her own actions. She braced herself, mouth opening as she scrambled for what to say.

Roland cleared his throat. "I thought this might be a diverting way to spend the rainy day," he said before Cassie could speak. "I set it up, and Miss Bell happened upon me. I invited her to join me."

Roland sent a warning glance Cassie's way, but she could hardly interpret it. What did he want her to say? *Should* she say anything?

Cassie felt as if an evergreen tree had fallen across her chest. She clutched her bow in both hands and focused on breathing. He was taking the blame for her, attempting to convince his mother this was all his doing. What had Cassie been thinking? The two of them had been alone for hours. *Again.* How could she have risked her reputation—*Vivian's* reputation?

"Miss Bell would do well to think twice before

accepting such an offer in the future." Mrs. Hastings's eyes narrowed as they flicked from Roland to Cassie and back again. She did not believe them, that much was obvious. But what could she do? She did not like Cassie. She would hardly demand Roland march her down the aisle when there were no other witnesses to their breach in conduct. "And perhaps she would refrain from aiming at me in the near future."

"It was an accident, Mother," Roland said.

"I am very sorry for the fright I gave you, Mrs. Hastings," Cassie quickly added.

Mrs. Hastings drew herself up to her full height. "Dinner is soon. I suggest, Miss Bell, you go upstairs to dress, or you'll be late."

"Of-of course," Cassie stammered. She nearly scurried out into the corridor before remembering she still held the bow. She turned back. Roland was already stepping forward, arm outstretched to take it from her.

"I am sorry," he murmured so his mother could not hear. "I will try to clear this up."

"Thank you," she whispered. "I did not mean to cause any trouble."

One corner of his lips curved up into a wicked grin. "And here I thought you liked a bit of trouble."

Cassie could not help the tiniest smile in return. He did not seem overly concerned. Perhaps he could set this all to rights. She bobbed a curtsy to both him and Mrs. Hastings and tried not to run as she left the ballroom.

CHAPTER 10

ROLAND WATCHED Miss Bell leave the ballroom, her skirts swishing around her ankles as her footsteps echoed in the quiet she left behind. There had been such panic in her eyes when he'd taken the bow from her. He wished he could have said more to reassure her, perhaps tell her what the afternoon had meant to him, even if it had ended badly. But with his mother present, he could not manage more than a few whispered words.

"Roland."

He faced his mother, who scrutinized him with very real worry.

"What were you thinking, being alone with that girl?" she asked. "Anyone might have happened upon you, and then what?"

He ignored her insinuation, though his stomach flipped at the thought. Couples had been forced to marry for far less. Yet he could not quite convince himself that would be so terrible a thing. With Miss Bell, at least.

"You mustn't blame Miss Bell," he said instead. "I take

full responsibility. And besides, I thought you would be glad to find me spending time with our guests."

Mother huffed. "Yes, perhaps I would have been a week ago."

"And what has changed? Did you not invite her for this very reason?"

She paced to the nearby window and looked out over the dreary, rain-soaked landscape. "I did, but now I am doubting my own judgment in regards to Miss Bell's suitability."

"Because of the incident with the painting?" He knew she would not like the question, but he had to know.

Mother turned sharply. "No. Well, not entirely. That, of course, did not endear her to me, but since then everything I have seen has only given me more qualms. She has acted more like her unruly sister than the proper miss I knew her to be in London, and I cannot account for it."

"Have you not thought to consider that is why I like her now?" he said. "I met her in London as well, if you'll remember."

Mother eyed him, as if fully understanding how careful she must be. They were at odds; they both knew that.

"I believe you think you like her," she said. "And I admit she is not the worst sort of girl you could marry. She is pretty enough, and from a good family. But she is not accomplished or poised or any of the things you need in a wife." She paused. "She is not the woman your father imagined for you."

Roland stepped back, jaw tight. Of course she would bring Father into this. "Not the woman Father imagined, or not who *you* imagined? Because if I remember correctly, he did not make me promise to marry a woman you approved of. He only wanted me to marry."

"Yes, but he hadn't any idea who you would set your sights on."

Roland shook his head. "You do not know the first thing about Miss Bell."

"And you know her so well?"

"Yes," he said simply. "I do. And since we've a week left to this party, I plan to use it as you intended: to see if Miss Bell is the woman I could spend the rest of my days with."

He strode past her and escaped to his study, where he could be assured of a few moments of peace before dinner. He paced before the window, the raindrops leaving wistful trails as they tumbled down the glass.

Why was Mother so against Miss Bell? Yes, the young lady had slighted her painting, but since then she had done everything in her power to win back his mother's approval. She had searched for that blasted cat, performed a song when she clearly had not wanted to, and been all that was kind and helpful. But Mother had seen none of that—only Miss Bell's apparent mistakes.

Roland wouldn't stand for it anymore. Not when he knew Miss Bell's—Vivian's—true nature. That she was thoughtful and interesting and intelligent, and that she only wanted to please.

And she was beautiful. He could not deny it. He leaned his shoulder on the windowsill, lost for a moment in the memory of those alluring blue eyes, her golden curls tumbling about her neck as she turned to look at him over her shoulder. He'd always thought Miss Bell pretty. But having come to know her better in the last week . . . Her character had become her beauty, more so than any dress, jewels, or rouge ever could.

He'd begun this house party so reluctantly that he could not believe he had reached this point.

That he could almost admit to having fallen in love.

Once Cassie made it to her room, she dropped onto her bed, her body overcome. The entire afternoon with Roland flashed through her mind—their conversation and teasing, his tempting nearness, and how little control she'd had over herself whenever he came too near. She hugged a pillow to her chest, trying to keep the heat there at bay, certain it would start a fire if she let it escape. What Roland made her feel, and the person she became when she was with him—she wasn't Cassie or Vivian. She was someone else, someone new. And she liked that someone.

Almost as much as she liked Roland.

Cassie groaned and buried her face in the pillow. The truth she'd been attempting to hide for days now stared down at her, like the hot sun in mid-July. What she felt toward Roland was not brotherly affection or friendly camaraderie. If she knew any better, if she'd had any experience whatsoever, she would even come close to calling it . . . well, love.

But she couldn't love Roland. It was impossible. *Vivian* was in love with Roland Hastings, and Cassie was just a poor substitute. She was not at all what such a man needed in a wife. He needed someone to help him further his connections, move upwards in society. Vivian would do that a thousand times better than Cassie ever could.

But that was beside the point. No matter what Cassie had imagined between her and Roland, it could never come to pass. She would never betray her sister, not when Vivian deserved every happiness, especially this one she'd long set her heart after.

And Roland . . . If the intensity in his eyes when he looked at Cassie was any indicator, then he felt something for her in return.

But the person he thought her to be did not exist.

Cassie managed her breathing, her head formulating a plan even as her heart struggled in vain to stop it. Vivian would be well in a day or two. Until then, Cassie would play a new part. The path she had been walking had proven too perilous. Now she would be careful. She could not avoid him completely, but neither would she seek him out or send him notes or exchange secret smiles with him.

That was for Vivian to do.

Cassie set her jaw. This was the right decision, for her, for Vivian, for Roland. She knew that. But the ache in her chest refused to dissipate, and she closed her eyes against the hot tears that fought to be free.

CHAPTER 11

MISS BELL WAS AVOIDING HIM.

Roland could easily tell, though she still smiled and conversed with the others that night after dinner as she always had. But when she looked at him, it was as though her eyes did not quite see him. Like he'd become an uninteresting painting on the wall or a statue gathering dust in the corner.

Had Miss Bell seen the risk they'd taken in the ballroom, and was she afraid to repeat it? Had her feelings changed? Or perhaps had the looming figure of his mother daunted her more than he'd realized?

The last was the likeliest. Mother was an intimidating figure even when one was not already in her black books. Everywhere Roland turned, Mother stepped in, remarking how pretty Miss Tindale looked or how neat Miss Marsden's needlework was. But not a word in favor of Miss Bell. In fact, not a word escaped his mother's mouth that indicated there was another young lady in the drawing room at all.

Roland wanted nothing more than to take Miss Bell aside and make her listen to him. She had to know that he did not care what his mother thought of her and that he only wished for her to be herself, forever and always.

But he did not want to push her. If she needed time, then he would be patient and understanding. Tomorrow would be a new day, and he would have his chance then.

When he awoke in the morning, the drizzle of rain had turned to spiraling white flakes that fell lazily to the earth, covering the grounds in a layer of snow. Mother was all enthusiasm, and she planned an entire day of snow-related activities: sleigh rides to the pond, ice skating, and hot tea when they returned.

Roland felt a lift in his heart. Snow was hopeful. Snow was renewing. And surely sometime in all the busyness, he would find a chance to pull Miss Bell aside and speak to her.

He waited at the base of the stairs as the party gathered in the entryway, all abuzz over the snow and the festivities. Miss Tindale found his side and chattered away, though he could hardly say what she spoke about. His responses were meager at best, and though he was sure he was being rude, he could not take his eyes from the top of the stairs.

But Miss Bell did not appear.

"Are we ready?" Mother adjusted the cloak around her shoulders. "Come then, the sleighs are waiting."

Miss Tindale looked up at Roland, no doubt expecting him to offer his arm. But he only stepped quickly to his mother's side, taking her arm before she could follow Mr. and Mrs. Marsden outside.

"What of Miss Bell?" he asked. "Are we not to wait for her?"

"She said she wishes to spend the day with her sister, who has been dreadfully lonely." Mother looked far too smug about her news.

"And I am sure you did nothing to discourage her," Roland muttered.

"What, dear?" She pretended not to have heard him.

Roland sighed. "I only asked after Miss Cassandra. Is she nearly recovered?"

Mother nodded as she eyed the footmen carrying their armfuls of furs and blankets to the waiting sleighs. "Yes, yes, the doctor was by again today. He says she'll be able to join us tomorrow."

How strange that would be, to have Miss Bell's identical sister at her side. Not to mention, it would be even harder to catch her alone.

Miss Tindale huffed as she moved past him and out the open door, clearly losing her patience with him.

"You have *other* guests besides Miss Bell," Mother said shortly. "You would do well to act as if you remember."

She swept after Miss Tindale, and Roland rubbed his neck. What a mess this was. How could he give Miss Tindale or Miss Marsden the attention they expected when he knew his heart was taking another path entirely?

He could be kind, at the least. Polite, but nothing more.

Roland glanced up the stairs one more time, as if Miss Bell might suddenly appear, her lips quirked in that inviting half-smile. But no one came. He took his hat from the footman and set it firmly on his head, determination growing inside him.

Miss Bell could try and avoid him, but he wouldn't let her. One way or another, he would find a way to see her.

Cassie crossed her arms as she stared out into the falling darkness, the twirling snow only barely visible by the flicking candlelight from their window. She'd watched the party return from their winter escapades not an hour ago, laughing and invigorated. In the twilight, she hadn't managed to pick Roland apart from the rest. Was he also laughing? Had he missed her today?

"Are you planning to dress for dinner soon?"

Vivian's voice stirred Cassie from her contemplation. She turned to her sister, wrapped in a blanket and seated beside the fire.

"No, I thought we could eat together, if you'd like." Cassie said, moving to take the chair beside Vivian. She'd already decided she would not go down to dinner. She had not the energy, not when she knew their charade was at an end. Dr. Duttle had come that morning, and he delivered the good news that Vivian had made a full recovery. Starting tomorrow, she was free to rejoin the party so long as she did not exhaust herself overmuch.

Cassie's end of the agreement was fulfilled. She had played Vivian as best she could, and now her sister could return to her place come morning. There was no point in going to dinner tonight.

It would only hurt Cassie more.

Vivian eyed her curiously. "Are you so weary of pretending to be me that you prefer even more solitude after an entire day together?"

"*Yes*," Cassie insisted. "Not only am I quite finished with this deception, but it has been too long since we spent any significant time together. And when you join the party tomorrow, I'll lose you once again."

Vivian reached over and took her hand. "You won't lose me, Cassie."

Cassie shook her head. "But I will. Or, at least, I'll lose what we have now. When you marry Mr. Hastings"—she nearly choked on the words—"things will never be the same. And I understand that is the way of life, but does that mean I cannot mourn the change?"

Vivian looked down. "There is no guarantee I'll marry Mr. Hastings. I hardly know the man, after all. What if—" She stopped, biting her lip.

"What is it, Viv?" Cassie asked, almost afraid to hear the answer.

Vivian exhaled. "What if I've dreamed up a future with a man who I have nothing in common with? What if we are not well suited once we come to know each other?"

Cassie swallowed. What could she say in response to that? She'd always thought Vivian's plan to romance Roland rather far-fetched, but now... In the last few days, Cassie could not deny seeing interest—and attraction, if she was not mistaken—in Roland's eyes when he looked at her. But *he* thought he was looking at Vivian.

"Do not be silly." Cassie forced a no-nonsense tone to her voice. "I have seen very clearly that Mr. Hastings and you have much in commone and will make an excellent couple. You needn't worry on that account."

Vivian squeezed her hand, a soft smile claiming her face. "I do not think I deserve to have you as a sister. I have been so focused on my future, on my own plans, that I think I have neglected you. But I shall try harder to show you I love you, no matter what may come. You have done so much for me."

Cassie swallowed. What had she done for Vivian, really? Made a mess of her reputation, abandoned her to spend time alone with Roland, and spun a web of lies.

"In any case," Cassie said, clearing her throat. "Let us spend the evening together without thoughts or worries for tomorrow. Just like we used to."

"Another round of backgammon, then?" Vivian suggested with a grin. "We are caught in a tie, and I should like to beat you soundly."

Cassie forced a laugh and moved to set the pieces again on the table. But her smile did not reach the depths of her heart, which felt more like the storm outside.

After another two hours of games and talking, Vivian declared she needed to rest in order to make the most of the next day. Even hard as it was to pretend nothing was wrong, Cassie far preferred the distraction of her sister to an empty room and wandering thoughts. But she could do nothing but bid Vivian goodnight and step out into the corridor, cold and lonely without the warmth of a fire. Cassie pulled her shawl more tightly around her shoulders and started toward her room.

"Miss Bell."

She froze, her hands gripping the loose ends of her

shawl. Not now. She turned slowly to see Roland stepping from the shadows, his dark, unruly locks falling over concerned eyes.

Cassie managed a quick breath, trying to reclaim her equilibrium. "Should you not be at dinner?"

"I pled exhaustion after the long day," he said, crossing his arms. "And I did not want to miss my chance."

"Your chance?"

"To intercept you before you hid away from me again."

"I wasn't hiding—"

He held up one hand. "I do not blame you in any way. I only . . ." He paused. "I missed you."

Cassie's heart thumped wildly, as if it might grow wings and burst from her chest. Roland had missed *her*.

He moved closer, the candlelight flickering over the lines of his face, his wide jaw and straight nose. "Come with me."

It was not a question but not quite a command. "Come with you where?" she whispered.

He smiled and held out his hand to her. "I believe it is my turn to surprise you."

Cassie stared at him, then his hand. She couldn't. She shouldn't. After what had happened yesterday in the ballroom, there was too much risk—both to her reputation and her heart. And what about Vivian? How could she think to—

"Please?" he said, his voice soft as the gently falling snow outside. She met his eyes once more, and the hope there destroyed all her defenses.

She slipped her hand into his.

His smile broadened. "I want to show you something."

He tugged her with him as he started down the corridor, and she needed no further encouragement. His firm, warm hand in hers sent continuous tingles up her arm and straight to her chest. One more night, she reasoned with herself. After all she'd endured in the last week, she deserved one more night of happiness. Then tomorrow . . .

But she would not think of tomorrow. Not with Roland guiding her through the quiet, dark corridors, and her pulse racing like a colt at Newmarket.

"Here we are," he finally said, pulling her to a stop outside an unremarkable door. She sent him a questioning look, but he only opened the door and ushered her inside.

A fire sparked in the grate across the room, leaving most of the room in shadow. Cassie moved to the center, turning to gain her bearing. A little bed near the window, neatly made. A row of tin soldiers arranged on a low table, and a shelf full of books and blocks.

"The nursery?" she asked in confusion.

Roland nodded. "My nursery, when I was a boy."

She managed a little laugh. "If you wanted to play soldiers, you only needed to ask."

He grinned. "I did not bring you here to play soldiers, though the idea is tempting." He moved across the room, waving her to follow him to the large window above a padded bench. He opened the window, and cold slipped into the room, surrounding her like the cool waters of the lake near Brightling.

She shivered as Roland turned back to face her. He grimaced. "I should have had you bring a cloak."

"Then I might not have come," she said dryly.

He chuckled, taking the blanket from the bed and coming to her. She inhaled a sharp breath as he wrapped the blanket snugly around her shoulders.

"How is that?" he asked, voice a bit gruff, his hands lingering along her bare arms.

She cleared her throat. "Better. Good." She was speaking nonsense.

He nodded and moved back to the window. "Come on."

"Where are we—"

But he did not wait for her to finish her question. He climbed through, ducking under the windowsill, then turned and offered his hand once again.

She could leave. Return to her room with her heart still intact. At least, mostly intact.

But she needed to know why he'd brought her here. She needed to know what here *was*.

She took his hand and stepped up onto the bench, holding the blanket closed with her free hand. He helped her over the windowsill and onto the small ledge below the window, which extended at a slight angle a few feet before dropping off. The snow drifted around them, though they were sheltered by the angle of the walls.

Roland helped her sit and then took his place beside her, one elbow propped on his upright knee.

"I used to sneak out here as a boy," he said, "to hide from my nursemaid, or whenever I felt particularly daring. I thought it might provide us an excellent view of the snow, since you did not go out with us earlier."

He spoke with no hint of judgment, but Cassie straightened. "I could see it very well from my window."

"That is hardly the same thing as experiencing it."

"No, this is much colder."

He laughed, throwing back his head. She could not help a smile as she watched him. She liked making him laugh. Usually only Vivian and Grandpapa laughed at her jokes; most others did not appreciate her humor.

"You cannot hate snow so much," he said, still chuckling as he gestured to the snowflakes swirling about in a complicated dance only nature knew.

"I do not *hate* it," she said, bringing her knees to her chest and wrapping her blanket around them. "But it is wet and inconvenient, and generally I prefer to be inside near a fire."

"And now?" he asked. "Would you rather be inside now?"

He was looking at her—she could see it from the corner of her eye. But she did not dare look back at him, knowing the strength of his gaze. "No," she said, focusing on the snow gathering on the roof just beyond her slippers. "No, I am quite content where I am."

They sat in silence for a long minute, the snow falling around them in a silent chorus. She could hardly feel the cold anymore, what with Roland's arm brushing hers.

"Will you tell me why you've been avoiding me?" he finally asked. "I've dared to guess that it involves my mother."

Cassie bit her lip. She hadn't thought she would see him again before tomorrow, and then only as Cassandra, not Vivian. She hadn't begun to formulate a response to such a question.

"I admit your mother is part of it," she somehow managed. "But it is far more complicated than that."

"Complicated how?"

She shook her head. What would he say if she told him the truth, that she was not the girl he thought her to be? That she had been lying to him almost their entire acquaintance? In fact, the only time she had *not* lied to him was when they'd first met in the corridor, their trunks switched.

"I am sorry, I should not press you," he said. "I only wanted the chance to . . ."

He paused, and then she did look at him. He stared steadfastly out into the snow, as if searching for the right words to appear.

"To what?" she whispered.

His eyes met hers, and Cassie had to gulp a breath. How could his eyes hold both such intensity and warmth?

"To tell you what I think," he said simply. "And what I think is that you should not care one whit what my mother says or believes. Because the reasons she has decided to dislike you are the very reasons I do like you."

Cassie did not move. Indeed, she *couldn't* move, not with his words still lingering in the air around her.

Roland turned so he faced her directly, stray snowflakes clinging to his dark locks. He slipped her hand from where she clutched her knees and held it in his, his thumb brushing over her knuckles. His touch seemed to melt her at every point, the cold and snow now distant, unimportant things in the face of his warmth.

"You are all a woman ought to be," he said, each word spoken carefully and quietly. "Compassionate. Sincere. Determined." He offered a smile. "You surprise me at every turn, and not just with archery ranges in the ballroom."

She gave a choked laugh, and he tightened both his hands around hers, warming them as if she held a fresh cup of tea. His scent surrounded her, impossibly masculine and enticing.

"You mustn't allow my mother's voice into your head," he said in a near whisper. "She has no place there, nor between us."

"But you cannot pretend she has no influence in your life," Cassie finally said with a catch in her voice. "I would not want to come between the two of you in any way."

Roland fixed her with a stern look. "I have yet to allow my mother to dictate my life, and I do not plan to start now. My choices are my own."

"I did not mean to say they were not," she said. "Only that . . . well, problems seem to follow me wherever I go. I have not made your life any easier since I arrived." It was the closest she could come to the truth. She *had* complicated his life, toyed with his emotions and desires. And he had no idea.

"No," he admitted, "my life has not been easier. But that has everything to do with an unwanted house party and nothing to do with you. Because you . . . you have made it all worthwhile." He raised her hand and pressed a soft kiss to her knuckles. A shiver swept across her. "You have made me remember what is possible, in life and love."

Love. Oh, he should not have said that word.

"Roland," she whispered. "I cannot . . . you mustn't . . ."

He silenced her protests with another kiss, this time on the soft skin inside her wrist. Her blood pulsed hot in her veins.

"Roland," she tried again, weakly.

Then she could speak no more, because he was kissing her. He pulled her close, wrapped one arm around her waist, the other behind her neck. But his lips—oh, his lips. They were everything. They explored and pressed and caressed, and she was so utterly unprepared for the dizzying swirl of emotion that swept her up. Cassie's arms wound about his neck, the blanket falling from her shoulders. Why had no one ever told her how absurdly wonderful kissing was? She kissed him back, not stopping to think, to doubt. She only knew she wanted this, more than she'd ever wanted anything—she wanted his kiss, his gentle words, his *love.*

His hands moved to circle her cheeks, leaving a trail of fire behind. She leaned into him, needing to be closer, and he responded with a new intensity in his kiss, an urgency that stole the breath from her lungs. But she did not pull away, not until he drew his mouth from hers, breathing deeply as he kissed her nose, her cheeks, her closed eyes.

"Vivian," he murmured.

Cassie's eyes shot open, and she jerked back, staring at him. *Vivian.*

He stared back, his brow furrowed. "What . . . what is wrong?"

Everything was wrong. Everything.

"I have to go." She scrambled to her feet, holding tight to the windowsill so she did not slip on the slanting roof.

"Let me help you," Roland protested.

But she clambered back through the open window without his help, barely finding her feet before stumbling toward the door.

"Vivian, what did I do?" He caught her, taking her arm before she could disappear into the dark corridor. "I'm sorry, I should not have kissed you like that. I thought you felt the same."

"I *do*," she said, the words tearing painfully from her throat. "I do. But you must let me go. Please. If you care for me at all."

He hesitated, still holding her arm. But she pulled away, and he let her go. She did not look back as she darted out of the nursery.

CHAPTER 12

WHAT A DISASTER. What an utter catastrophe. Why on earth had she gone with Roland tonight? She had known it would only lead to more heartbreak, and yet she had followed after him without question. She had hurt him, and herself, in the process.

And what was she to tell Vivian? How could Cassie face her, knowing she'd kissed the man her sister hoped to marry? Surely she had broken every rule of sisterhood. She was only meant to distract Roland, not *fall in love with him*.

Her eyes burned with tears, but she swiped at them angrily, refusing to let them fall. She did not get to cry, not now. Not after what she'd done.

"Miss Bell."

Cassie came to a sudden halt, nearly tripping over her own feet. Mrs. Hastings stood in the corridor ahead, still dressed in her evening finery.

"Mrs. Hastings," Cassie stammered. "Is dinner over already?"

"Quite," she said. "Hardly reason to prolong such an event when my son did not even bother to show for it."

Cassie said nothing, only tried to control her frantic breathing. But Mrs. Hastings moved closer, her narrowed eyes roving over every inch of Cassie's face.

"You were with him again, weren't you?" she asked quietly.

Cassie clenched her jaw. She might have made a mess of everything, but she did *not* owe this woman any answers.

"I see." Mrs. Hastings stopped an arm's length away. "At least you are smart enough not to admit it."

Hostess or not, Cassie was finished with this conversation already. She was finished with this entire evening.

"I beg your pardon, Mrs. Hastings," she said stiffly. "I am tired, and I am going to bed. Good night."

She moved around the older woman, and she had nearly made her escape when Mrs. Hastings called after her. "Oh, Miss Cassandra?"

"Yes?" Cassie said shortly, spinning back.

A look of victory spread across Mrs. Hastings's face, and Cassie realized her mistake.

"I knew it," Mrs. Hastings breathed. "I knew you were the wrong sister."

"No," Cassie said, her voice weak. Her mind would not work; her breath caught in her lungs. "No, you do not understand. My sister truly is ill, and she—"

"I do not care that she is ill," Mrs. Hastings said shortly. "I only care that she is not *you*. I haven't the faintest idea what drove you to take her name in the first place, but Roland never need know."

Cassie shook her head. The woman was making no sense.

"My son thinks he is in love with you." Mrs. Hastings approached slowly, her eyes fixed on Cassie. "But of course, that is only an illusion. We both know you are not right for him, for this life. You could never be what he needs. Could you mingle with the highest of society? Stand beside him at balls and dinner parties, ready to help him make his way in the world?"

Cassie clutched a hand to her stomach, the roiling there so intense she thought she might be sick.

"No," Mrs. Hastings said. "No, you could not. You would embarrass him, and yourself."

"What do you want from me?" Cassie finally said. "What would you have me do?"

"Switch places again." Her voice grew cold. "I would prefer he marry into another family altogether, but Roland has shown no liking for the other young ladies I invited. He is already in love with who he thinks is Vivian Bell, so that is who we will give him."

Switching back had always been Cassie's plan, the goal from the start. But now that she knew her intentions lined up so neatly with Mrs. Hastings's, she felt a forceful resistance to it. Why should this woman gain everything she wanted when she'd only made Cassie's life miserable?

"And me?" Cassie asked, gritting her teeth. "Shall I simply fade to the background, pretend as though nothing happened?"

The matron seemed to hesitate for a moment, then she set her jaw. "No. I would have you leave altogether. Your being here would only complicate things. We will say

Cassandra's condition was not improving and she wished to recover fully at home."

Cassie turned away, hugging her arms tight around her chest.

"You know this is the right thing to do." Mrs. Hastings almost sounded sympathetic. "I always intended your sister for Roland, not you. You were never more than a placeholder."

Why did she have to be right? Cassie knew it to be true. But a voice inside begged her to reconsider, to imagine the possibilities. She could tell Roland everything, admit to Vivian what had happened. She'd never intended to fall in love, after all. It had been an accident. But could Roland love someone who had deceived him so completely? Could Vivian ever forgive her?

She took a shuddering breath. No. It was useless. She could never hurt her sister like that. And *if* Roland had begun to see her true self, and perhaps even care for her, Mrs. Hastings was right. Cassie could never be a proper wife to him. Not like Vivian could. She had to give Vivian and Roland the best chance at happiness possible. It was all she could do to make amends for her deception. The two of them would be well-suited, undoubtedly. She loved them both, so how could they not love each other?

Cassie turned back to Mrs. Hastings. "I will go," she said softly. "In the morning. Roland will never know." And Vivian would never know Cassie's true feelings.

Mrs. Hastings nodded. "I'll have a carriage readied for you at first light."

Cassie nearly thanked her, an instinct from years of etiquette lessons. But she bit her tongue.

Mrs. Hastings took a step away and then paused. "I did not want to hurt you," she said, almost seeming to mean it. "But it is for the best."

For the best. Cassie could not be there a moment longer. She spun on her heel and ran until she found the safety of her room, the quiet crackling of her fire.

She did not bother to call for Jennings to help her pack. After lugging her trunk to the base of her bed, she opened it and began tossing in dresses and shawls haphazardly. Everything would be dreadfully wrinkled, but that hardly topped her list of concerns at the moment.

After emptying her wardrobe, she moved to her desk. Upon seeing her package of cherry comfits, Cassie's will nearly broke, remembering Roland's gentle teasing. But she squared her shoulders and tossed the package into her trunk. She would throw them out when she arrived home.

When there was nothing left in her room save for a traveling dress for tomorrow, Cassie stood with her hands on her waist, breathing hard, fighting the tightness in her lungs. But she couldn't fall apart now, not when one task still remained—the most difficult of all. She sat at the writing desk and pulled out a piece of paper.

So much had happened since she'd come to Hartfield, and soon this house party would be nothing more than a memory, bittersweet and inescapable.

"Leaving?" Vivian had been inspecting herself in the vanity mirror, but now she spun to face Cassie, the morning light illuminating her wide eyes. "What do you mean, you are leaving?"

Cassie sat on the bed, one hand steadying herself on the bedpost. She had to be convincing. "I am tired, Viv. Of the pretense. And you know I have never enjoyed parties. Now that you are better, there is no reason for me to stay. I can go home for Christmas."

Vivian shook her head. "But I need your help. What if Mr. Hastings mentions something you haven't told me about your time together? What if—"

"Everything you need to know is in here," Cassie said, pulling the letter from her reticule. "Read it, please, and all will be as it should."

Vivian took the letter, but her eyes did not leave Cassie's. "What happened?" she asked quietly. "Something has changed since last night."

Cassie sighed. "I have simply had enough of this house party and want nothing more than the quiet seclusion to which we both know I am better suited."

"You know I do not believe you in the slightest," Vivian said, crossing her arms.

Cassie gave a sad smile. "Of course. But I also know what I am doing, I promise."

Vivian looked far from convinced, but Cassie did not want to give her any more chances to argue. She went to her sister and embraced her. "I wish you every happiness with Mr. Hastings," she whispered. "He is a good man, and I know you will be happy together."

Vivian pulled away, her eyes glossy with tears. "I hope so, but I do not think I shall ever be truly happy until you are settled and content as well."

Cassie shook her head. She was quite cried out, having shed more than her fair share of tears during the long night. "You may be wishing for that a long while yet." Vivian frowned, but Cassie did not want to prolong this conversation any more than necessary. "Goodbye, Viv. I hope to hear good news from you soon."

Vivian kissed her on the cheek, and then Cassie hurried from the room, down the stairs, and out the front door, where a coach awaited her. The footman helped her inside and closed the door behind her, the thud echoing in her ears with resounding finality.

She looked back at the manor as the coach started away, as if she might catch a glimpse of Roland at a window, or riding from the stables. But she saw no one.

Cassie curled into the corner of the coach, her eyes unseeing as they drove through the snowy landscape. Surely Vivian was reading the letter now. Cassie had tried her best to explain all that had happened between her and Roland. She'd written of their late-night conversation in the alcove, the archery range in the ballroom—and their kiss on the roof in the snow. She could hardly keep all that a secret now, not when Vivian needed to know everything.

She'd written that she'd been too embarrassed to tell Vivian all this in person, and that of course Roland had only kissed her because he believed her to be Vivian. There was no doubt in Cassie's mind, she'd said, that Roland Hastings loved Vivian Bell.

The only thing she did not tell her sister was how much Cassandra Bell loved Roland Hastings.

Cassie closed her eyes, remembering briefly those few

moments of bliss from last night, when Roland had kissed her.

When she'd felt absolutely and completely loved.

CHAPTER 13

Roland did not sleep.

To be fair, he did not really try. He sat before his fire for hours, poking at the ashes as his memories wound about in circles. Vivian, her cheeks rosy and eyes bright, looking up at him. The sweetness of her lips on his, her soft hair and skin. And then the look of utter panic that had overtaken her features as she scrambled back through the window.

Away from him.

And yet.

And yet he clung to what she'd said, that she *did* feel the same way toward him. Had he simply pushed too far, too fast? He hadn't meant to kiss her. He'd only wanted to talk. But how was he supposed to resist her sitting there beside him in the snow, impossibly beautiful, unreasonably adorable?

He could not begin to explain his actions to himself, let alone to her. This house party was to have been a thing to endure, but he could never have anticipated Vivian.

He'd fallen for her so quickly—though *falling* was not the right word. He'd plummeted into love. Plunged. Really, it was his own fault she'd run off. First his mother's actions and now his impulsive kiss.

He needed to fix this. He needed to reassure her he did not expect such ardor in return, even if his heart was already hers. He would give her the time she needed to decide.

The ashes of his fire were nearly cold when sunlight began drifting through his curtains. Roland dressed and escaped for a ride, hoping to cool the fever that had taken control of his body since last night. When he returned, he paused in the entryway when he heard female voices coming from the parlor. Was Vivian inside? How might she react to seeing him?

He took a deep breath. They would see each other sooner or later, and perhaps it was better to do so in a group setting. He only wanted to show her that his affections remained unchanged despite her reaction last night.

Roland stepped inside the parlor and stopped short. Vivian sat across the room, dressed in a pretty pink gown, her fair hair glowing in the sunlight. But that was not why he stared. Vivian sat beside his mother, and both women were *smiling*.

Mother looked up. "Ah, there you are, Roland. We thought you'd deserted us again."

Her pointed slight at his missing dinner last night barely registered in his mind. He focused instead on Vivian, who stood upon his entering. She clasped her hands tightly, her blue eyes fixed on his.

"Good morning, Miss Bell," Roland said quietly. "I trust you slept well."

She nodded. "Yes, very well, thank you."

There was something strange in her posture—her shoulders were too stiff, her back as straight as the arrows they'd shot in the ballroom. But of course she would be ill at ease, considering their meeting last night.

"Won't you join us?" Mother asked, smoothing her skirts nonchalantly. "The others are still eating breakfast, but I am sure they will come in soon."

Roland glanced at Vivian, hoping for some indication as to whether she wanted him to sit with them. She nodded without hesitation. "Yes, please join us. Your mother has been telling me amusing stories from your childhood, and I should so like to hear your side of them."

Feeling somewhat reassured—she hadn't run away, at least—he pulled a chair closer to them and sat beside Vivian.

"And what mistruths has my mother been telling you?" he asked. "Surely not the story about the grasshopper again."

Mother gave a titter. "How can I not share that one? You decided my sewing basket would make the perfect home for the creature, and forgot to mention that fact to me before I discovered it inside!"

Vivian laughed, but it was not the unbridled, joyful sound he'd come to expect from her. No, this laugh sounded forced, practiced almost. But then, they *were* seated beside his mother. He could hardly expect her to act as she did when it was just the two of them.

"I would have been so affrighted to find a grasshopper

among my thread," Vivian said, leaning forward. "I admit I have no fondness for wildlife."

"Save for cats," he said with a grin, hoping to put her at ease.

"Cats?" she repeated.

"And parrots, of course." A hint of his confusion found its way into his voice. Did she not want him to discuss such a thing before his mother?

"Oh. Of course, parrots." Vivian gave a sudden nod, as if recalling a long-forgotten fact. "My grandfather has one, though I would not advocate it as a proper pet."

"Decidedly not," Mother said. "But I am glad to know you have a fondness for cats, considering my own."

"Y-yes," Vivian stammered. "I adore cats. They are quite . . . pretty."

Something was not right. Roland squinted at Vivian. Nothing she had said was wrong, but it was more *how* she said it.

"Is your sister joining us today?" Roland asked, watching her closely. "I hope she has made a full recovery."

Vivian blinked rapidly, as if she'd gotten something in her eye. "No. No, I'm afraid Cassandra has decided to return home. She is feeling better, but not yet up to enjoying the house party."

Roland nodded. "Ah, a pity I did not get to spend much time with her. But perhaps I shall send her a package of cherry comfits to assuage her disappointment."

"Comfits?" Vivian furrowed her brow. "An interesting gift. Very . . . thoughtful. I am certain she would be glad to receive it."

He stared at the young lady before him, at her carefully folded hands, her pursed lips, and her guarded eyes. The golden curls and blue eyes were the same, but nearly everything else was different.

And then it all connected in his head, his thoughts flying faster than a sparrow on the wind.

"You are not Vivian," he said slowly.

Her mouth parted, but she did not speak.

Mother gave a nervous laugh. "Of course this is Miss Bell. Who else would it be?"

But Roland shook his head. "This is not the woman I spent the last week with."

Mother stood, face reddening. "Roland, you are being ridiculous, and quite rude to Miss Bell. I insist you apologize—"

"No." The young lady stood as well, and Mother gaped at her. "No, please do not apologize. You have nothing to feel sorry for, while I have everything to regret." She took a deep breath and looked Roland straight in the eye. "I *am* Vivian Bell, but not the one you came to know. That was my sister, Cassandra."

Cassandra. Her name repeated in his mind, again and again.

"She pretended to be you?" he asked, perplexed. "Why?"

Mother sat again, holding a hand to her forehead, but Vivian did not look away from him, though her cheeks grew pink.

"I . . . I am embarrassed to admit I formed an attachment to you during our time in London. When I grew ill during our journey here, I begged her to take my name

115

and—" She closed her eyes tightly. "I asked her to ensure that the other young ladies did not monopolize your time."

Roland leaned back in his chair, head spinning. His memories skimmed over the last week; he remembered all the little oddities and inconsistencies he'd noticed in Miss Bell—Cassandra. Her competitiveness with Miss Tindale, her apparent battle within herself to appear more proper than she was. And her *singing*.

Then, to everyone's surprise, including his own, a short laugh escaped him.

"This explains so much," he said, shaking his head. "In truth, I cannot believe I did not guess it sooner. I simply assumed she acted strangely because she was nervous." Another realization struck him, and he turned to his mother. "Nervous of *you*, Mother. Tell me you did not know about this."

Her face paled. "No! Of course not." She paused. "That is, until last night."

Roland narrowed his eyes. "What happened last night?"

"I . . ." She swallowed. "I may have encouraged Cassandra to return home. I thought it best, considering her entire character was a deception from the start. But Miss Bell here—"

"That was *not* for you to decide, Mother." Now Roland was on his feet. He turned to Vivian. "Miss Bell, I am certain you are all that is sweetness and gentility, but—"

"But you are in love with my sister," she said softly, understanding growing in her eyes.

Roland hesitated. He did not want to hurt this lovely

young lady, when she was guilty of nothing but setting her sights on the wrong man.

"It is all right." Vivian looked down at her clasped hands. "After spending just a few minutes with you, it is quite obvious how you feel about her. I had my suspicions after reading Cassie's letter this morning, but I wanted to see the truth for myself."

"She wrote you a letter?"

"Yes, explaining all that happened." She cleared her throat. "And now I must be clear about a few things. Cassie is my dearest friend, and I have no doubt it was her sincerity, her cleverness and compassion, that endeared her to you." She took a steadying breath. "If there is any chance Cassie returns your feelings, then you must go to her."

Roland forced himself to breathe, memories from last night on the roof slipping through his confusion. Miss Bell—Cassie—returning his kiss before running away. He understood now why she'd done it. She hadn't wanted to hurt her sister.

He stepped forward. "Where is she now? You said she decided to go home."

"Yes." Vivian's smile faded. "She left early this morning. It is a two-day journey."

He strode to the window, inspecting the ground. It would not be easy traveling in the snow, especially once it began to melt and mud took its place. But surely he could make better time on horseback than by coach. If he hurried, perhaps—

"Roland."

His mother's voice snapped him back to attention. She stared at her hands, held tightly in her lap.

"Roland, I . . ." She shook her head. "I thought you were making a monumental mistake, and I saw it as my duty to correct you." Mother finally raised her eyes. "Cassandra Bell is not who I would have chosen for you, but if she is who you want, I will resign myself to it. She is determined and intelligent, and that will have to be enough."

That was as close to an apology as he had ever heard from his mother. He nodded, though far from ready to forgive her completely. "If she will have me."

"You will never know," Vivian said, "if you do not give her the chance."

Roland inhaled an unsteady breath. Was he ready to propose? Not even a fortnight ago had he considered such a thing possible.

But Cassandra had changed all that. Her ringing laugh danced through his mind, her gentleness and her spirit, the ease with which they conversed for hours on end. And he knew this was what he had been searching for. What his father had wanted for him.

He looked at Mother. "Father would have liked her," he said softly.

Her eyes misted, and she turned away. "Then what on earth are you waiting for, my boy? Go and claim your lady."

He turned to Vivian, his mind racing. She raised her chin, though a flash of pain still echoed behind those familiar blue eyes. "You must go," she said, her voice firm. "That is my wish for you, and for Cassie."

He stood still, trying to grasp all that had happened in

the last few minutes. If he knew anything about Cassandra, it was that she cared for her sister above all else. It would be no easy task to convince her to accept him when it might injure Vivian.

Roland looked at Vivian. "I do not wish to take advantage of your kindness, Miss Bell, but if you are willing, I would be grateful for your help with something."

She pulled back her head in surprise, but then she nodded. "Of course, Mr. Hastings. Anything."

CHAPTER 14

CASSIE HAD EXPECTED some relief upon arriving home, but the sight of the familiar columned portico and brick exterior of Brightling Place brought her nothing but emptiness. That and exhaustion, of course, after two days of bumping around in a carriage with nothing but her thoughts for company.

The footman helped Cassie down from the coach. There was no snow here at Brightling, nothing to hide the depressing drabness that was December. She climbed the front steps, pulling at the ribbons of her bonnet as she stepped inside. "Mama?" she called. "Papa?"

Their front hall was not so grand as Hartfield Court's, but neither was it small enough that her voice would not carry to wherever her parents might be. She frowned, handing her things to the footman.

"Cassandra? Is that you?"

She did not think there was anything that could make her smile at the moment besides her grandfather's voice. Cassie hurried to the study, which Grandpapa claimed as his refuge. He sat in his great leather armchair, the same as always: a glass of whiskey in one hand and a book in the other, his disorderly gray hair at odds with the tidiness of his clothing and those sparkling blue eyes.

He set down both the glass and the book at her appearance, his eyebrows raised. "Cassie?"

"I am sorry to intrude upon you, Grandpapa," she said, her voice breaking. "I know you did not expect me for another few days."

"Never mind that." He stood and moved toward her, his face crinkled in concern. "What is wrong?"

She shook her head fervently. She could tell no one what had happened, not even her grandfather. There could be no chance the truth would make its way to Vivian.

"Nothing," she said brightly. "Just a long journey, that is all. I grew bored of the house party, and Vivian was getting on well enough, so I decided to return for Christmas." She forced a smile. "I know how you love Christmas."

"That I do." Grandpapa scrutinized her, then pulled her into an embrace. "I missed you, child. Your parents are dreadfully dull company without you and Vivian around."

Cassie managed a laugh. "And where are they? They haven't abandoned you?"

"I could only dream," he said, pulling away. "No, they've gone to town for some errands. I expect them back soon."

Cassie nodded. She could tell her mother she had done everything in her power to give Vivian the match she'd dreamed of—even if it had broken her own heart in the process.

"I'll have the maid bring us tea." Grandpapa moved to the door.

"I can do that," Cassie insisted.

"No, no," he said hastily. "You stay here. Keep Arnold company."

She hadn't noticed the parrot in the corner of the room, quiet as he was. Usually the creature squawked constantly and made a great deal of noise, but today he was quiet.

"Stay here," Grandpapa said again, a strange look in his eye.

Cassie furrowed her brow. "All right."

He disappeared without another word. Odd. He must really have missed her.

Cassie wandered to the fireplace, warming her hands as she took in the comforting adornments of her grandfather's study. The rows of books, the paintings featuring sights from all over the world, the broad windows that let in the waning afternoon light. She let out a long breath. At least she was home.

"Mary."

Cassie spun before she realized it was not a real voice. It was only Arnold in his cage, stretching his bright-red wings. She went to him, head tilted.

"Mary?" she repeated. "Have you finally learned a new word, then?" Or a name? Perhaps they had acquired a new maid in her absence. Mother had been searching for one when they'd left for Hartfield Court.

"Mary," the parrot squawked again. "Mary."

Cassie smiled faintly. If nothing else, she could spend her Christmas entertained by this silly parrot and her loving grandfather. She would need such distractions, dreading as she was the news that would surely come from Hartfield soon. Cassie bit her lip, fighting her own mind from turning where she knew it should not turn—back to Roland.

Footsteps sounded behind her, and she cleared her throat against the persistent lump there. She did not want Grandpapa to suspect anything.

"It seems Arnold has made some progress in my absence," she said, trying to mask the hoarseness in her voice as she reached a finger inside the cage to stroke the bird's tail feathers. "But who is Mary?"

A sigh and a short laugh. "I should have believed your grandfather when he said it was useless."

Cassie stiffened. That was *not* her grandfather.

Pulling her fingers from the cage, she swallowed, then turned slowly to peek over her shoulder. Roland stood just inside the door, hands clasped behind his back, a half smile toying with his lips. She stared at him, all of him, from his polished boots to his dark hair. It *was* him, wasn't it? Surely she wasn't so desperately in love as to imagine him.

"What—" Her voice cracked, as if she were again performing at the pianoforte. She tried again. "What are you doing here?"

"I admit you posed an interesting challenge, leaving hours before I did." He moved further into the room, his eyes never leaving hers. "It meant a late night and an early morning, but I managed to arrive about two hours ago."

Cassie gripped the back of her grandfather's armchair to steady herself. What was happening? He should be in Hartfield, with Vivian.

"I know everything," Roland said softly.

A new panic gripped her. Did he know who she really was? Had he discovered her deception and come to punish her for it?

"I know," he said, his voice full of meaning. "I know you are Cassandra Bell. I know you pretended to be your sister for the entire house party."

Cassie took a sharp breath. "Roland—"

"I know you kept the truth from me, even after it became clear there was something between us."

"I am so sorry—"

"And," he interrupted, "I know you only did so with the best of intentions. To help your sister."

She blinked. He smiled and stepped closer.

"I know that, despite your name," he said, his voice quiet and sincere, "you are the same woman I talked with for hours. You are the same woman who reassured an anxious cat and who performed the worst rendition of a carol I've ever heard."

Roland took two more steps to her side, holding both her hands in his, pressing them against his chest and warming them.

She finally found her voice. "But I deceived you. I made you believe I was Vivian."

He shook his head. "I would not care if your name was Hildegard. A name does not a person make."

She wanted to smile at his jesting, but her unbelieving

heart did not allow it. Cassie closed her eyes. "You did not have to come all this way."

"Actually, I did. But you were right, the blasted parrot is completely useless. We—meaning your grandfather and I—finally convinced the creature to say one of the necessary words, but now it seems to be the only word it knows. And truthfully, I first thought to come on Christmas, like my mother suggested. But I simply could not wait."

Cassie opened her eyes again. "You must know I haven't the faintest idea what you are talking about."

"Marry," Arnold squawked again.

And then she understood.

"Marry me," Roland said quietly, his eyes searching hers. He pulled her closer, still holding tight to her hands. "I have been searching for you for a year, and now that I have found you, there is no hesitation in me. I want you by my side, just as I want to be at *your* side, always."

Cassie gaped at him, surely the most unbecoming prospective bride in all the world, with her mouth wide as a saucer. Marry him? Her mouth fought to form the word she wanted so desperately to say. But she could not say yes. Not now.

"I cannot," she whispered. "If you know why we switched, then you must know I could never hurt my sister."

Roland's expression shifted, and a gentleness claimed his eyes. He pressed a kiss to her hand. "I thought you might say something like that." He reached inside his jacket and withdrew a folded note.

She took the note with a trembling hand and opened it.

Cassie,

There is no doubt in my mind that you would do anything to ensure my happiness. Now you must let me do the same for you. Please, be happy.

All my love,
Vivian

Cassie exhaled a shaky breath. Oh, Vivian. She must have written this note even as her own heart broke.

Roland's warm hands came around hers, still holding the note. "Vivian," he said quietly, "understands completely. She told me the truth herself, and she told me to come here."

Cassie lowered the note and set it on the nearby table. She could only imagine the selflessness of her sister to make such a choice.

"She wants this for you," he said. "But you must decide if this is what *you* want."

"But . . . but your mother," she protested. *Why* was she speaking of his mother? "How will this ever work?"

He grinned, a slow spread of his lips that brought flutters to every inch of her body. "There is a reason dower houses are built, Cassie."

Cassie. *Cassie.*

She could not have stopped herself if she tried—and she certainly did *not* try.

Cassie propelled herself upward and kissed him with such force that he staggered back a step. But then he caught her in his arms and kissed her back, his lips firm and demanding against hers. Every emotion she'd felt since leaving Hartfield came roaring through her, channeling into this moment, this kiss. Her heart pounded furiously in her chest, as if shouting aloud that it had been claimed, and her hands wandered from his chest to find the scruff of his neck, rough after two days of travel. She quite liked that, and she pulled herself even closer. His arms tightened around her, his hands exploring her waist and back.

It wasn't as though she hadn't enjoyed their first kiss on the roof. But *this* kiss was so much more—it was confirmation of all she'd convinced herself she could not have. From the moment she'd met Roland, she'd fought every rush of attraction and every meaningful connection. Now she felt it all, deep in her soul. She was meant to be here, with Roland.

Still wrapped in each other's arms, they shared one more slow, tantalizing kiss. A blissful sigh escaped from Cassie, and she felt Roland's lips curve upward beneath hers.

"That was my way of saying yes, in case you were uncertain," she whispered.

"Really?" he teased. "I thought perhaps we'd stepped beneath some mistletoe."

She smiled and pulled back slightly as her fingers toyed with the hair at the nape of his neck. "I must clarify one thing, however."

"And that is?"

"We will *not* be naming any children Hildegard."

He laughed, drawing her hand to his lips and kissing it twice. "You shall have no argument from me, I assure you." Then he gave a dramatic exhale. "Now, I am certain your grandfather is waiting to hear the good news."

Cassie grinned. "He can wait a few minutes more. I think you are quite right about the mistletoe, and we should not risk any bad luck."

Roland grinned back. "If you insist."

His expression softened, and he turned her chin up with gentle fingers. Cassie slid her hand up his forearm, not looking away. She hadn't even realized she'd wanted this—love and marriage—until she had it. Until it was solid and absolute. And knowing she had Roland, that he loved her and wanted her in return, was more happiness than she'd thought to imagine for herself.

"I love you, Roland Hastings," Cassie whispered. "I thought you should know."

He swallowed, then bent again slowly and met her lips with impossible tenderness. Cassie leaned into him, into the comfort of his arms and the promise of their future.

EPILOGUE

TWO YEARS LATER

"THEY ARE HERE!" Cassie exclaimed as she clattered down the grand staircase of Hartfield Court. "Roland, they're here!"

She'd spotted the two coaches from an upstairs window as she'd overseen the preparations in the guest rooms—ensuring each had a roaring fire in the grate and extra blankets to keep out the December chill. It wouldn't do for Grandpapa to catch a cold, after all. She had been efficient and organized as she worked, as any hostess for an upcoming house party ought to be, but upon seeing the tops of the coaches traveling above the eastern hedge, she'd lost all sense of propriety and had run from the room and down the stairs like a schoolgirl.

"Roland," she called again, nearing the bottom of the stairs. "Where are you?"

"What's all the fuss? Are we being invaded by the French?"

Roland's deep voice came from back up the stairs, and it so startled her that she nearly tripped down the remaining few steps. She caught herself on the banister and spun to see him standing at the top of the staircase, his handsome face changing from amusement to concern.

"Are you all right?" he asked, starting down after her.

"Of course I'm all right," she said, beaming up at him. "I just spotted their coaches on the road."

His concern fell away and his eyes warmed. "Ah," he said as he approached. "I was wondering. I haven't seen you run that quickly since you smelled Cook baking her apple tarts."

"You are terribly funny," Cassie said dryly. "Quite hilarious. Now come along, they'll be here any minute."

"Any minute?" He came even with her on the stairs, a wicked grin lighting up his face. Before she could react, he trapped her against the banister, his arms on either side, and leaned in close. Cassie could not help a little sound of surprise as her heart beat faster.

"In that case, I must take this last opportunity before we are overrun," he said, his deep voice husky in her ear as he pressed a light kiss to her jaw. "I can't very well be kissing you all around the house as I am wont to do."

"I suppose not," Cassie said, delightfully breathless. His nearness and warmth had yet to lose their potency in the last two years. "Though I daresay they know how marriage works."

"Yes, well, not *our* marriage," he said with a chuckle. "A man must have some secrets from his wife's family."

He kissed her, the lines of his body pressing against hers, familiar and thrilling all at once. His hands slid behind her, pulling her away from the banister and more firmly against him, and his impish lips did their job a bit *too* well. Cassie was thoroughly lost in their kiss until the sounds of crunching gravel and horse hooves met her ears.

She pulled back abruptly and slapped Roland lightly on the arm. "Do contain yourself, good sir. I have been planning this party for a month and I am determined that it go well."

He lifted one eyebrow playfully. "Is that why you made certain my mother would be visiting her cousin before extending your invitations?"

Cassie narrowed her eyes. "No. That was simply a happy coincidence."

He laughed, pressing one last kiss to the barely-contained smile on her lips. "As you say, my dear."

In truth, Cassie would not have minded so terribly if the elder Mrs. Hastings *had* remained at the dower house through the party, and would have even invited her to join the festivities. Her mother-in-law certainly had opinions and disliked when anyone disagreed with her, but the two of them had found a balanced peace since Cassie and Roland's marriage two years ago. The birth of twin girls last December, Tabitha and Flora, had gone a long way to heal any past hard feelings. But then, who could possibly resist the charms of baby laughs and deliciously dimpled elbows?

"Are the girls sleeping?" she asked as Roland offered his arm and they made their way to the marbled floor of the entryway.

"It took nearly an hour, but they settled eventually," he

said with exasperated pride. "How they have so much energy in such small bodies is beyond me. I do not think we are paying the nursemaids enough."

They went out the front door as two footmen hurried to open the doors of the waiting coaches. The winter wind blew fiercely, throwing Cassie's hair into disarray as she and Roland stopped at the top of the wide steps. She pushed her curls from her face with impatience, trying to maintain a calm composure, but when Vivian stepped down from the first coach, Cassie could not have stopped her reaction for a thousand pounds.

"Vivian!" She ran to her sister, throwing her arms around her. Vivian caught her with a laugh, embracing her in return. It had been nearly five months since they'd last seen each other, an unendurable amount of time, in Cassie's opinion.

"Oh, you are here," Cassie said joyously, tightening her hold around her sister's neck. "Finally, you are here."

"I won't be here much longer with you choking me," Vivian managed, though she grinned.

"Ha," Cassie said even as she pulled back. "No one hugs you like I do, you know that."

"Save for her husband, perhaps?" came a playful voice from the coach.

Cassie furrowed her brow in pretend contemplation as she turned to face the fair-haired, thick-jawed man now stepping down from the coach. "Hm," she said with a dramatic sigh. "I suppose in the absence of one's dearest sister, a husband is an adequate substitution."

Mr. Parker was quite used to Cassie's teasing and only grinned, calling up to Roland coming down the stairs behind her. "Did you hear that, Hastings? We are forever relegated to second place."

Roland laughed. "Oh, that is hardly news to me. I learned this quite early in our marriage. I had often heard about strong bonds between sisters, but no one warned me about *twin* sisters."

"Quite right," Vivian said, linking her arm with Cassie's and pressing a kiss to her cheek. "It is good that they know their places."

"Could *our* places possibly be inside out of the cold?"

Cassie spun at Grandpapa's voice and, finding his twinkling blue eyes and wild gray hair, practically launched herself at his middle.

"Heavens," he said with a laugh. "Any harder a hit than that, and we might inform the military we have a new weapon akin to cannons."

"You all may tease me as much as you like," Cassie said, her voice smothered in her grandfather's coat. "But you shan't bring down my spirits. Not today."

Mother and Father also approached from the second coach, greeting her with sweet embraces and warm words. Since her marriage to Roland, Cassie had seen a softening in her mother that she could never have expected, and their relationship, while still growing, had become something she treasured dearly.

"Come inside," she called out, leading Mama by the elbow. "Before Grandpapa freezes all the way through."

Everyone laughed and talked over each other, and there was a great commotion as they all went into the grand entryway, removing their cloaks and great coats, hats and bonnets.

"There's tea in the drawing room," Cassie said above the bustle. "I'm sure you all could use a hot drink."

Mother fixed her with a stern look. "Do you think we came all this way to have tea? No, dear, I am a grandmother first. Where are my darlings?"

Roland wrapped an arm around Cassie's waist. "Napping, I'm glad to say. The nurses are quite worn out, and—"

"Mama!" came a happy, high voice.

Roland sighed. "Well, we *hoped* they were napping, at least."

The whole group turned to look up the stairs as the two nursemaids appeared holding Tabitha and Flora, their cheeks red and golden hair tousled. Cassie could not help but smile at the sight of the girls, though she knew they needed a much longer nap if they were not to be grumpy later this evening. She could hardly be surprised, though. No doubt they'd sensed her restless energy all day and could not bear to be left out of the fun.

"I am sorry, Mrs. Hastings." Mary, the senior nursemaid, looked contrite as she brought Tabitha down the stairs. "They woke each other up and then there was no getting them back to sleep."

"Oh, you needn't worry," Cassie said, taking Tabitha from her arms. Her daughter was wide-eyed as she took in their guests. She'd met them all before, of course, but the memory of a one-year-old was not long. She curled against Cassie's shoulder, tucking her face away shyly.

"Mama!"

That was Flora again, now reaching for Cassie from

the other nursemaid's arms. Her voice had an almost petulant tone to it, her eyes a familiar bright-blue.

"This one," Roland said, intercepting the nursemaid and scooping Flora from her arms, "always dislikes when Mama gives Tabitha too much attention." He tossed the girl into the air and she shrieked in delight.

"Well, they both shall have plenty of attention in the next fortnight," Vivian said, smiling indulgently. "With both grandparents, a great-grandfather, and an aunt and uncle, I daresay they will never be set down once."

"Then they certainly will never learn to walk on their own," Cassie said with a laugh.

"They can walk when we leave," Mother said, coming to her side and holding out her arms to Tabitha, who only buried her face more fully in Cassie's shoulder. "Oh, none of that, my dear. Look, I've brought you a gift."

She enticed Tabitha to part from Cassie with the help of a tiny wooden rattle, beautifully carved with birds and trees, and soon was walking her about the entry, pointing out various things as Tabitha watched with serious eyes. That, of course, meant that Flora only screeched louder for Cassie, who gave a resigned sort of laugh as she took her other daughter from Roland and balanced her on her hip.

"Heavens," Vivian said, eyes dancing as she watched Cassie. "Was this what it was like for Mother when we were younger?"

"If so," Cassie said, "then I suddenly feel a great deal of remorse for all our childish pranks."

"Surely not *all* of them." Roland elbowed her. "Your fondness for switching places, for example?"

Cassie cast Vivian an exasperated look. "I do not think he will ever stop teasing us about that."

Though Vivian may have once blushed in embarrassment, since her marriage to the ebullient Mr. Parker, she more easily took the teasing in stride.

"Careful what you say, Mr. Hastings," she said now. "I should hate for you to eat your words when Tabitha and Flora are old enough to cause true mischief."

"Especially," Mr. Parker added, placing a hand on his wife's back, "since we will soon be adding our own mischief-maker to the brood."

Cassie gasped, clutching Flora tighter, her eyes fixed on Vivian. "You are expecting?"

Vivian slapped at her husband, though her eyes shone with delight. "I thought we were to announce it after we were settled, you rascal."

He only pressed a kiss to her temple with a grin. "I waited as long as I could."

"Oh!" Cassie hurried to her sister, throwing an arm around her even as she still held Flora, who squawked in protest at being squashed against Vivian's shoulder. "Viv, how could you not write to me?"

Vivian laughed, pulling away and smoothing Flora's hair. "I've only known a few weeks, and I was determined to tell you in person."

Mother, Father, and Grandpapa watched with beaming smiles, no doubt having already heard the news before arriving.

"How do you feel?" Cassie asked, examining her sister's face. It was perhaps more rounded than the last time she'd seen her—a good thing, she thought. Cassie's own pregnancy had taken a toll on her those first few months, and she'd found it difficult to keep any food down at all.

"A bit ill now and again," Vivian admitted. "I can hardly complain, knowing what sickness you endured."

"Tell her what the doctor said," Mr. Parker urged.

"What?" Alarm surged inside Cassie. "What has the doctor said?"

Vivian set a soothing hand on her arm. "It's nothing to fear."

Cassie looked between her sister and Mr. Parker, brow furrowed. They exchanged a smile.

"The doctor believes," Vivian began, "based on my measurements—and he cannot be certain, mind you—that I am carrying twins."

Cassie gaped, frozen in shock. She could not have heard right. It did not seem possible. *Twins?*

But Roland reacted plenty for the both of them. He gave a great laugh and pounded Mr. Parker on the back. "You simply had to show us up, did you?" he said cheerfully.

Mr. Parker grinned. "Yes, yes, that was the plan all along."

"Twins," Cassie repeated, still staring at Vivian, her sister smiling gently. Then her vision blurred, her eyes filled with sudden tears. "Oh, Viv, it is too wonderful."

"I've heard that the tendency towards twins is passed through the maternal line," Mother said knowingly. "So it makes a great deal of sense, really."

Grandpapa laughed. "I do not think you truly care

how it came about. You are only glad for more babies to dote upon."

Mother waved him off, though the pleased look in her eyes was admission enough.

"Twins," Vivian said again, taking Cassie's hand. "Imagine them all growing up together, cousins so close in age."

"Imagine if they are all girls," Roland said with false horror. "Four little miscreants running about, exchanging identities and causing a ruckus."

Cassie beamed, her throat aching from restrained tears, her voice too far gone to summon. As her family chattered on around her, as Vivian took Flora from her arms and hugged her, as her home was filled with laughter and love, Cassie could only watch with an overwhelming joy.

"I do hope those are happy tears," Roland said, his arms circling about her waist and tugging her back against his chest.

She shook her head, swiping at her watery eyes. "You know they are. You know how happy I am."

"Are you?" he asked, his jaw brushing against hers as he dipped his head. "Are you happy, my dear?"

She turned, and despite her entire family standing within view, she pressed a sweet and lingering kiss to Roland's lips. "Beyond measure," she whispered. "Beyond belief."

And he kissed her back, leaving no doubt in her mind that he knew precisely what she meant.

ALSO BY JOANNA BARKER

The Havenfield Series

The Truth About Miss Ashbourne (Book 1)

Otherwise Engaged (Book 2)

Standalone Novels

Miss Adeline's Match

Secrets and Suitors

A Game of Hearts

A Heart Worth Stealing

Novellas/Anthologies

Beauty and the Baron

Romancing Her Rival

All Hearts Come Home for Christmas

I would love to keep in touch! You can connect with me on Facebook and Instagram (Author Joanna Barker). To join my newsletter, check out my website, www. authorjoannabarker.com. If you enjoyed this book, please leave a review! Thank you for reading!

ABOUT THE AUTHOR

Joanna Barker firmly believes that romance makes everything better, which is why she has fallen in love with writing Regency romances. When she's not typing away on her next book, you'll find her listening to podcasts, eating her secret stash of chocolate, or adding things to her Amazon cart. She thinks being an author is the second-best job in the world—right after being a mom. She is just a little crazy about her husband and three wild-but-lovable kids.

Printed in Great Britain
by Amazon

35405778R00085